Jane Blonde

spylets are forever

JILL MARSHALL

MACMILLAN CHILDREN'S BOOKS

First published 2009 by Macmillan Children's Books
a division of Macmillan Publishers Limited
20 New Wharf Road, London N1 9RR
Basingstoke and Oxford
Associated companies throughout the world
www.panmacmillan.com

ISBN 978-0-330-45813-9

1 3 5 7 9 8 6 4 2

A CIP catalogue record for this book is available from
the British Library.

Typeset by Nigel Hazle
Printed and bound in the UK by CPI Mackays, Chatham ME5 8TD

jill marshall moved from the United Kingdom to New Zealand, along with her small daughter and her even smaller mad dog. Her childhood ambition was to become an author, so in 2001 Jill gave up her career at a huge international company to concentrate on writing for children. When not working, writing and being a mum, Jill plays guitar, takes singing lessons and is learning to play the drum kit she has set up in the garage. One day she might even sing in a band again . . .

Look out for the brand-new book from
Jill Marshall:

Doghead

Books by Jill Marshall

jane blonde, sensational spylet*
jane blonde spies trouble
jane blonde, twice the spylet
jane blonde, spylet on ice
jane blonde, goldenspy
jane blonde, spy in the sky
jane blonde, spylets are forever

*also available in audio

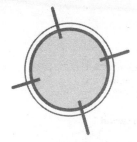

for my jane blonde birth partners –
glenys, emma and especially rachel.
thank you just isn't enough.

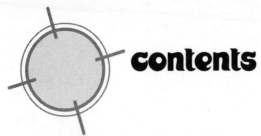

contents

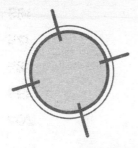

**are we not drawn onward, we few,
drawn onward to new era?**

midnight mates

Janey Brown had been having a dream – a very nice one in which she was playing tennis with her dad. Boring, perhaps, to anyone else, but to Janey it had been the best dream ever. Her dad had been just that – a dad. Not a spy. Not an ever-changing personality who invented a pretend brother and then many different machines so he could live his extraordinary life. And definitely not someone who had turned himself into a hairy caveman and then lost himself in time. She sighed. Why did she have to wake up now?

Struggling out of bed, she peeped out of the window, wondering if it was the moans and howls of the ferocious gusts of wind outside that had woken her. A storm was brewing, although the day had been close and hot. An Indian summer – that was what her mum called the unusual autumn weather.

From the darkness appeared a face. 'Aha!' whispered Janey. So it wasn't just the gale that had woken her. It must have been her spy instincts kicking in. Janey drew back behind the curtains, then moved alongside the window.

She'd been trained well. *Surprise, surprise, surprise* – the first rule of spying. G-Mamma had taught her that right back at the beginning. So instead of doing the obvious thing and looking through the crack in the middle of the curtains – risking being spotted – Janey hopped up on to the edge of her bed and peeked down through the narrow gap above the curtain rail. The face appeared disembodied, bobbing around in the alley behind the house like the moon on a stick. But that was only an illusion. The spy – for that was obviously what it was – was simply dressed in black so his body wasn't visible in the darkness.

Furthermore, the spy was friend, not foe. Janey relaxed and twitched the curtain to one side.

What was Alfie up to? It was after midnight. And even though it wasn't that unusual for Spylets like herself and Alfie to be galloping about the globe in the middle of the night, that was only when they were on a mission.

She watched as Alfie jumped over the back fence, catching his trousers on a jagged splinter. He dropped down, head swivelling left and right as he took in the details of the garden.

Janey opened the window. 'Halo! What are you doing?'

Alfie stared back at her, his upturned face glowing

in the moonlight. For a moment he looked terrified, then he grinned, holding up a scrap of paper that was nearly snatched from his hand by the wind.

'What's that? And what are you wearing?' hissed Janey.

Janey only ever saw her best friend and Spylet buddy in one of three outfits: his school uniform, his denim-blue SPIsuit, or jeans and a sweatshirt. Oh, and occasionally his football gear. Right now he was sporting wide black trousers that billowed around his legs – no wonder they'd snagged on the fence – and a short V-necked black jumper that made him look taller and more gangly than usual.

Alfie glanced down at his clothes, then shrugged. Style was never that important to him. The little tornado behind him made his whole body quiver, and Janey tutted as she realized what he'd been up to. He'd been flying the Pet Jet. And he'd left the engine running, so much so that some sort of force was dragging him back towards it.

'Hang on,' whispered Janey. 'I'm coming down.'

Moments later she eased open the back door and flitted silently into the garden. 'Alfie, why didn't you just . . . ?'

. . . SPIV me, she had been about to say. He could easily have contacted her on the SPI Visualator she always wore around her neck or kept on the bedside table at night.

But he wasn't there. Janey pushed back the mousy hair that whipped around her face as the gathering storm grew more violent. Head down, she battled through the wind towards the back of the garden where Alfie had been standing.

Gone.

'Alfie!' said Janey crossly. She could have just stayed in bed. What was he mucking about at? The wheel of the Pet Jet was still spinning.

Maybe he was hiding. A glint of moonlight caught her eye as she looked for him behind the garage. When she had finally made up her mind that he wasn't there, Janey braved the gusts of wind and foraged in the grass for whatever had gleamed.

It was a little glass ball, clear for the most part, with a curved sliver of coloured glass nestled at the centre. For a moment Janey wondered if it was one of G-Mamma's sweets. She'd been living in the garage for a while, after all, and the ball could be a re-invented Malteser that had been through the Wower. But then she spotted a strand of black fibre attached to it.

'Alfie's.' It had probably fallen out of his pocket when he'd caught his new black trousers on the rotting fence.

Well, I might just keep it, she thought. Serve him right for getting me out of bed on a hideous windy night. And Jane Blonde stomped her way across the garden and headed back to the warmth of her duvet.

The wind swooped and roared throughout the night, but with a pillow wrapped around her head Janey hardly heard a thing.

marble marvels

'Don't forget your English homework,' called Jean Brown as she hurried around the kitchen, packing lunch boxes with one hand as she emptied compacted dirt out of the vacuum cleaner with the other. Janey wouldn't have been at all surprised to find dust bunnies in her sandwiches instead of cheese and pickle.

'I've put it in my bag,' said Janey, whisking her lunch box out of her mother's grasp. 'And you should slow down.'

Her mum sighed. 'I would love to. Honestly, with SPI and Clean Jean to manage, I'm finding it all a bit much.' She slammed shut the little trap door on the vacuum cleaner. 'But Uncle James is hovering more and more, asking me why I'm not putting one hundred per cent into the business – keeping his eye on the books and all that. I can't really tell him it's because I'm also looking after my missing husband's spying organization, can I?'

'Suppose not,' said Janey.

She felt rather like sighing herself. Not long after getting her father back at the end of their last adventure, he'd turned into a caveman and disappeared down the centre of one of his own gadgets, the Rapid Evolution machine called the R-Evolver. G-Mamma was half managing Solomon's Polifical Investigations for Boz Brilliance Brown, Janey's super-SPI dad, and helping out with the Clean Jean business, while Janey's mum was trying to be big-boss Clean Jean, Gina Bellarina (super-SPI) and just plain Jean, mum of Janey, all at the same time. Everyone else had either vanished or was so busy that they might as well have gone too.

It seemed very unfair on her poor, overworked mum. 'I don't think Uncle James should be nagging you.'

Janey's mum gave her a tight smile. 'It is his job. Organizing money – it's all he cares about. But I probably need someone to keep me in check. Hold it all together. Just until . . .'

'I know, Mum.' Janey gave her mum a hug, trying not to cry. 'We'll find him. We'll get him back. I promise.'

Jean just nodded, her face a bit wobbly, as Janey heaved on her heavy backpack and set off for school.

At least Alfie was his usual self. Possibly not even busy *enough*, judging by his midnight meanderings in her back garden. He got on the school bus two stops after her, and waved, but the aisle was too packed with giggling, gabbling schoolkids for him to join her. Janey nodded, then angled her hand towards her chest, index and middle finger in an inverted V. To any non-SPIs catching the signal, it would look as if Janey was attempting a sort of rapper greeting, but Alfie knew what it meant. She was pointing to the SPI-buy under her jumper. *SPIV U later.*

They needed their spy gadgets these days. It wasn't anywhere near as easy for them to communicate at Everdene School as it had been at Winton. They weren't in the same form, and only came together once a week for music in the school hall. Janey always enjoyed those classes – for one, she was able to stand next to Alfie, and sometimes she could even help him with the dreadful wailing he called singing.

Besides that, she really liked the school hall. At one end stood a large stage from which the headmaster boomed out his pronouncements in assembly, and at the other hung long wooden boards detailing all the former students who'd been Head Girl or Boy, or gone on to get a university degree. Janey hadn't been at all surprised to see the name Maisie Halliday, Alfie's mum, picked out in gold lettering as a former Head Girl, with the exotic sounding 'Jakobi Delacroix' as Head Boy in the column beside her. Janey loved it all, as she loved the old grandfather clock in the foyer and the mysterious, creepy stairs leading up the headmaster's office. The whole place had a sense of history, a feeling

8

of being where past and present met, and Janey felt as though she fitted in.

Tuesdays were easy – maths, science, music and PE. Even sports was better at Everdene, although Janey suspected that might have something to do with the fact that she sneaked her Fleet-feet on under her socks. She had to wear extra big trainers to accommodate them, and the Fleet-feet didn't work as well as when they made direct contact with the ground, but they allowed her to keep up with the rest of the class in cross-country and spring high enough to look naturally good at gymnastics. She'd even been put forward for the school athletics team for long jump, which had made quite a few people look at her differently.

Now, still glowing from playing hockey on the sports field, Janey jostled her way in next to Alfie as music class began and pressed the little glass ball she'd found into his hand.

'Yours, I think,' said Janey.

Shielding it from prying eyes, Alfie peeked down at the ball. 'Oh,' he said, surprised. 'Thanks.'

'What is it?'

'It's a marble,' said Alfie, pocketing it. 'It was this game they played a million years ago when Mum was young, knocking out other kids' smaller marbles and so on. She says she collected them. I reckon she just confiscated them off the other kids and kept them for herself.'

Janey grinned. 'Well, I very nearly kept that one. You should be more careful.'

'What did . . . ?' started Alfie, but a frantic rattling of the music stand by the teacher stopped him in his tracks.

'Halliday!' snapped Mr Young. 'There's no Mummy Halliday for you to run to here, you know.'

'Sorry,' muttered Alfie, turning scarlet as people whipped round to look at him.

'Detention after school.'

Janey almost winced for Alfie, but she managed to keep her face neutral. She knew only too well what it felt like to be singled out at school, and everyone staring only made matters worse. As soon as the teacher had turned away to rifle through his book, she made the *SPIV U* sign again and faced the front sharply. Alfie's question – and hers – would have to wait. Meanwhile, she blocked off her hearing as Alfie proceeded to drone his way through 'We Plough the Fields and Scatter' and the school day ground to a close.

Her mum was still out when Janey got home, so she wandered up to G-Mamma's Spylab, newly refurbished in shades of lilac, pink and white.

'Ho there, Spygirl,' called G-Mamma, knitting furiously, as Janey stepped off the SPIral staircase into the room.

'Gosh,' said Janey. 'I would never have thought knitting would be your thing.'

G-Mamma sniffed. 'Don't look down your nose at arts and crafts, Janey baby,' she said, frowning as she picked up a dropped stitch. 'You'd be amazed what you can do when you're good at dressmaking and a bit of the old crochet. Watch this!'

She cast off her knitting with a flourish, and Janey studied the straggly scrap of yellow wool hanging from her SPI:KE's hand. 'It's for Trouble,' announced G-Mamma, scooping up the Spycat.

'Oh. Is it a . . . scarf?'

'Scarf? Laugh Out Loud!' hollered G-Mamma. 'It's his new tail.'

Janey gasped as G-Mamma sashayed across the Spylab to the Wower and prepared to chuck Trouble and the scrappy knitting inside. It was quite possible that Trouble would emerge like a soft toy, knitted from head to toe, with bits of stuffing hanging out. On the other hand, thought Janey, he did need a new tail since he'd lost his proudly cultivated golden one in a tussle with a pterodactyl.

'Wow and Weld,' called G-Mamma, tying the knitting to Trouble's back end and shoving him into the spy shower with a firm spangle-shod foot. 'Sort that tail out!'

The door clanged shut. Almost immediately there came the unmistakable hiss of spy-transforming steam, accompanied by a rather startled yowl. G-Mamma held on to the Wower door as it rattled on its hinges, and then glanced at her watch. 'That's it. Time's up. You're cooked, puss.'

She threw back the door, and from the Wower vapour emerged a magnificent sight: Trouble marched out with his quiff held high, his emerald eyes pulsating and glowing, go-faster stripes resplendent along each furred side, all capped off by a tail to end all tails. It was as golden as his original one had been, but somehow each long strand of wool had separated, stood on end and fanned out, so that Trouble now resembled some mythical creature . . .

Half cat.

Half golden peacock.

'Wow,' breathed Janey and G-Mamma together. Trouble just sniffed, flipped his enormous tail backwards and forwards, then snapped it shut as he curled up at Janey's feet.

'Ha! I have . . . *excelled* myself!' squealed G-Mamma, grabbing the rest of the wool. 'Imagine what I could make for myself! Eyelashes like . . . caterpillars. No more mascara! Waist-length hair. No. Why stop there? Knee-length hair. FLOOR-length hair. Yes!'

Before her SPI:KE could disappear into the Wower with her knitting needles, Janey said, 'That all sounds great, G-Mamma, but I'm not sure it would be very practical.'

G-Mamma stopped dead. 'But . . . Oh, I suppose you're right.' Her face fell, then brightened. 'Wait!

What about wigs! G-Mamma, Wig Wonder of the World.' She could obviously picture it already, and her face folded into pre-rap rapture. 'That's it. Listen!

> *'Your little head still feeling bare?*
> *Just get G-Mamma's Wonder Hair!'*

Janey smiled. 'I don't think you need a new business, G-Mamma,' said Janey. 'What with Dad lost in time, and Mum trying to run two different organizations, you're more than busy enough. Any . . . any progress on finding Dad?'

Janey hardly dared to ask. The R-Evolver was possibly the most complex and frightening piece of machinery that her father had ever invented, and G-Mamma was being rightly cautious in finding out exactly how it worked before sending anyone through it.

The SPI:KE sighed, her enormous gold SPIV rising and falling on her chest. 'Well, I've spun the R-Evolver both ways on the Pet Jet,' she said. The R-Evolver was currently masquerading as a spare wheel on the fighter plane in the allotment behind the garage. 'And I keep chucking things into the middle of the tyre, hoping something will show me what to do. No luck so far.'

'What have you put in it?'

G-Mamma ticked the items off on her fingers.

13

'A book. An apple. A doughnut. Chinese takeaway. A SPIsuit, in case it reaches your father. Newly knitted jumper, in case he's cold.' She held up a skein of fluffy orange wool, a colour Janey knew her dad would never wear in a million years. 'And then I threw a plate in. For his takeaway.'

'And nothing's come out again.'

G-Mamma shook her head, then jumped up. 'Oh, apart from this. I think it must be a bit of the book. I found it this morning next to the R-Evolver.'

Janey took the scrap of paper from between G-Mamma's electric-blue fingernails. She studied it carefully, turning it over to look at the front and the back, and frowned. 'It doesn't make sense.'

They both stared at the printed paper. There was just one word on it, in large, bold type:

EMOCME

'This doesn't look as though it came from a book,' said Janey. 'If it did, there'd be some sign of words around it, or printing on the back.'

'Maybe the R-Evolver changed it somehow.'

'Or maybe,' said Janey, getting excited, 'it's a message. A code! Something from Dad.'

'In that case, brainy Janey,' said G-Mamma, 'what do you think it means?'

But just then the SPIV on the chain around Janey's

neck buzzed, and Janey remembered something. 'Alfie,' she said as soon as her friend's face appeared on the SPIV screen, 'that marble I gave you in music . . .'

Alfie's face paled, reliving the trauma of the music class. 'Oh, right, thanks for reminding me,' he said bitterly. 'How embarrassing was that?'

'Did you also drop a note when you were in our garden last night?'

'What are you talking about? I thought that marble was a present. A present that got me into detention, I might add. And why would I have been in your garden?'

Janey held her breath for a moment, then gazed at G-Mamma over her flashing knitting needles. 'In that case, Agent Halo,' she said carefully, 'I think you'd better make sure you're here tonight. Because some Spylet boy – who looks remarkably like you – is leaving us messages. Be here at midnight.'

'Right, and if I get another detention because I'm exhausted in the morning . . .'

'Just have a Wower.'

'All right,' said Alfie reluctantly, but Janey could hear the tinge of excitement in his voice.

She knew just how he felt. Something was happening. Something unusual. And Jane Blonde was on the case.

sub on no bus

'Blonde,' barked G-Mamma through the crack in the back of the fireplace, 'I don't think we need to wait until midnight. Come see.'

It was barely ten thirty – pretty early by SPI standards.

'It's got to be Alfie,' Janey grumbled as she clambered through the fireplace tunnel to the Spylab. 'He's come here early just to catch me out.'

'There's something going on at the bottom of the garden,' said G-Mamma, peering through the Ultra-gogs perched on the end of her nose. They looked very out of place with her pink bunny-eared sleepsuit.

'Keep watching.' Janey whisked through the Wower as quickly as possible, barely taking the time to enjoy the robotic hand smoothing her tousled hair or the tingling transformational Wower drops that smoothed out every angle and jangly nerve until she was once more the living and breathing ace Spylet, Jane Blonde.

In less than ninety seconds she sprinted to G-Mamma's side in her SPIsuit, her Blonde ponytail and her own Ultra-gogs firmly fixed in position. 'It's hard to see, isn't it? It's so windy again . . .'

'There!'

G-Mamma pointed to the Alfie-sized figure that had appeared in the alleyway. Once again he looked left and right, his hair blasted by the wind. But this time he didn't leap over the fence. Instead he took a quick peek at a scrap of paper pulled from his pocket, then ran off down the alleyway towards the street.

'It's the boy from last night!' said Janey.

'Quick! He's disappearing!' G-Mamma zoomed in with her Ultra-gogs, hopping from one fluffy foot to the other. 'The wind's dropped. Off you go!'

'I don't think that was the wind, G-Mamma,' said Janey as she opened the window. 'It's the blast from the Pet Jet. I think this kid's been using the R-Evolver – maybe he's come from the past!' Janey grabbed her ASPIC from the industrial-looking wall that groaned with gadgets and all manner of spy vehicles – Back-boats, ISPICs, SPI-cycles, Fleet-feet, eSPIdrills, SPISegs . . . and her own beloved Aeronautical SPI Conveyor: slender; silver; superb.

'Right, here I go. G-Mamma, you check around the Pet Jet for clues.' Janey pushed off along the counter and braced herself for the vertical drop down the side of the building, face down.

The ground rushed up to meet her, and Janey transferred her weight to the back of the board, tilting it so it slid above the grass on its cushion of air. Behind her, G-Mamma fell out of the window in a fuzzy tumble, but managed to right herself and land upright, then bounce off at an angle across the garden. With Fleet-feet on its soles, it seemed the pink bunny suit was not just for sleeping in.

'Track and Trace,' said Janey to her Ultra-gogs, hovering for a moment over a footprint in the alley. Her spy glasses whirred away, emitting a satisfying click as soon as they established a clear print in her right lens, and then they were off, scanning ahead of her, zooming in on identical footprints wherever they fell – in the flower bed at the corner of the house, under the nearest street light, across the road at the bus stop . . .

'Next one,' ordered Janey as the whirring and clicking came to a halt. The Ultra-gogs panned up and down the street, but came up with nothing except the distant tail lights of a late bus. Suddenly they clicked insistently.

'He got on the bus? No way. What kind of spy does that?'

But the Gogs zoomed, focused and X-rayed, and, sure enough, there on the back seat, in the very place that she and Alfie always tried to sit on the way to school, were the dark hair and square-set shoulders of the mystery boy.

Janey reached for her SPIV just as G-Mamma shouted her name and popped into focus. 'Blonderini, you were righty almighty. The R-Evolver wheel on the Pet Jet was still spinning, and there are footprints right underneath it.'

'Well, whoever it was who hopped out of the R-Evolver just rode away on the number 93 bus.' Janey rubbed her nose, perplexed. 'Where's he going?'

And they both realized the answer at the same moment: 'Everdene.'

The 93 night bus only had one stop – the road on which her school was situated. She'd better check it really wasn't Alfie, planning a late-night prank. 'Al Halo,' she called into her SPIV.

The screen showing G-Mamma miniaturized, and Alfie's bleary-eyed features appeared. 'Is my watch wrong? I only make it elevenish.'

'Where are you?'

'Er, in my bedroom.'

'Show me.'

'What?' With a resigned sigh Alfie pointed his SPIV at various objects in his room, including the maths homework on decimal places that had sent him to sleep.

'So it's definitely not him, Blonde,' said G-Mamma, making Alfie jump. He stared at his SPIV suspiciously.

Janey explained quickly. 'Alfie, something's

going on. I'm going up to the school; G-Mamma, you keep staking out the Pet Jet in case he comes back. Alfie, would you mind the Spylab while there's nobody there? I don't want to disturb Mum.'

'Be there in two minutes,' said Alfie, alert again.

Janey pushed off. It was much further to Everdene than it had been to Winton School. Clinging to the shadows of the walls, Janey hopped off and on her ASPIC, Fleet-footing over the more clearly lit parts, where she might be spotted, until finally, puffing slightly, she reached the road the school was on. The Gogs started whirring again, picking out footprints that had made their way right up to the locked school gates! After a quick check that nobody could see her, Janey took a run-up, bounced on the balls of her toes and vaulted the iron spikes with a tight handspring.

The school seemed much creepier at night. Suddenly the strange tales Janey had heard – of murders on the headmaster's staircase and ghosts appearing from the belly of the clock as it struck midnight – didn't sound so ridiculous. She used the diamond on her spy ring to cut a small pane of glass from a classroom window and wriggled through. No sign of anyone at all.

She crept out into the foyer, the yellow clock face glowing eerily in the shaft of moonlight reflecting off Janey's SPIsuit. 'Ugh.' She shivered. It was the first time she'd noticed that the dial was golden, almost sun-like, and she couldn't help but think of her arch-enemy, Copernicus, and his vile Sun King mask. But when she looked more closely she saw that the picture on the clock depicted the phases of the moon. She was just peering at it more closely when suddenly the minute hand clicked round to the eleven thirty position and there was a loud *DING* from the clock's depths.

'Argh!' The shock had nearly blasted her out of her SPIsuit. Janey leaned over on to her knees, panting. Get a grip, Blonde, she told herself. Then the Ultra-gogs let out a click that was almost as loud as the clock's chime. Another footprint!

But just the one. 'Trace.' Janey turned her head to help the Gogs, but still there was no satisfying *beep* to tell her which way to go. 'But that's silly. Where did he go?'

Swivelling her feet around, she stood on the muddy footprint. It pointed straight ahead. And straight ahead was . . . the grandfather clock.

Janey took a deep breath and turned the tiny key in the clock's narrow door. It swung open, and she almost laughed at herself. There in front of her were two metal rods with enormous brass weights on the bottom, swinging in combination with the central pendulum, and various cogs and wheels. What else had she expected?

She was just about to close the door and set off down the corridor when the glasses focused on

21

something inside the clock. On the wooden base of the clock innards, there was half a footprint. Just the heel. The toe had disappeared into what appeared to be a solid piece of oak.

'Aha!' cried Janey. She pressed the back panel of the clock, but it stayed firm – even after a whole minute's pushing and shoving. But then the image of her fireplace tunnel appeared in her mind. That didn't respond to brute force either. It opened only when someone pressed on a particular spot in the ten-past-two position.

And here she was in front of a clock. 'Worth a try, anyway.' Janey reached out a finger and touched the face of the clock directly on the number two. A little circle of glass pressed down beneath her fingertip and with a gentle sigh the back of the clock eased open. Janey grinned in disbelief. She waited until the pendulums swung to their highest point on either side, then jumped through the inverted V.

She was on a staircase. The narrow steps doubled back on themselves, and Janey stopped, disorientated. 'Map of school,' she whispered to her Ultra-gogs. The floor plan pinged into life on her left lens, a little silver X marking where she stood. Under the foyer. Past the assembly room. Treading carefully along the earth floor, Janey moved down the slender passage beneath the corridor . . .

Until she reached an office – a small underground office, situated under the stage of the main hall.

And sitting at the desk was the boy she'd thought was Alfie. Actually he looked a lot less like him close up. He was slightly older, for a start, and broader across the shoulders.

He was watching her carefully, as a hunter might watch his prey. Or rather . . . rather as if he himself was the prey, thought Janey.

'Who *are* you?' he said.

Janey felt for the passageway behind her, in case she needed to escape. 'I'm Jane, Jane Blonde.'

The intense eyes rested on her ponytail and then shifted to the piece of paper in his hand. 'Then you're the one,' he said.

Janey's heart skipped a beat. 'What do you mean?' Instinctively she dropped into a combat position. Prepared to fight. For her life, if necessary.

The boy flicked back to the paper. 'Jane. The one who knows. Ponytail. Funny clothes.'

'The one who knows what? And your clothes are a bit weird too, if you don't mind my saying.' Janey held her ground. 'Who are you?'

The boy stood up slowly and held out his hand. 'Hello, Jane. I'm Sol. Solomon Brown. I've been sent to find you.'

And Janey realized in an instant why she'd recognized him, why he seemed so familiar.

The boy was her father.

spyclops

'Sol . . . Solomon Brown?' Janey stared at the hand he'd extended. No missing fingers yet. Somehow she was face to face with her own father as a boy – before experiments, before SPI, before . . . before Janey even existed.

Solomon lowered his hand, wiping it awkwardly on his trousers.

'Sorry,' said Janey, embarrassed. 'Er . . . hi.'

The intelligent eyes watched her carefully the whole time. 'So you knew about the den,' he said quietly.

'Den?'

Janey looked around. There was a primus stove in one corner and an odd assortment of broken cups, and the desk was strewn with papers. Pinned to the upright wooden posts that held up the stage were a number of drawings, complicated images with mathematical formulae scribbled all around: the Crystal Clarification machine, a Wower and a Satispy transporter, and a strange picture of what looked like a tall column with a fat tyre wrapped around it. Across the top someone had written, in heavy print:

THE R-EVOLVER

Her breath catching in her throat, Janey felt a little dizzy. This wasn't just a schoolboy den. This was . . . the very first Spylab. The place her father had been coming to in secret all his life. No wonder the ten-past-two position had worked!

Solomon moved in front of the wooden post, obscuring her view of the diagrams. 'How did you know this place was here?'

'It's the first time I've ever seen it. I followed you,' said Janey.

The boy squinted disbelievingly. 'But I came on the bus. How could you track me down that quickly?'

He doesn't know, Janey realized with a strange lurch of her heart. Even though Sol would come to invent all these things, from the plans and drawings fluttering across the desk in the draught from the secret corridor, this boy didn't yet understand about gadgets that would become his very own SPI-buys.

And finding it all out could blow his mind. She'd have to tread carefully.

'I know, it all seems amazing,' she said softly. 'But I can show you. May I?'

Solomon stood aside a little reluctantly, and Janey pointed to one of the pictures. 'That's the R-Evolver. I think that's how you travelled here in the first place, isn't it, when you jumped out of the wheel of the fighter jet in my garden?'

Solomon stared, and then nodded. 'It was unreal. Completely unreal. I still don't understand what happened – all I know is I was sent here to grab some papers from this den. And to find you.'

Janey swallowed hard. 'You travelled through time. That's what happened. Now you're in the future – in a time when these ideas for inventions have been developed. They allow me to run really fast, and Track and Trace with my glasses, and . . . well, all sorts of things. Look.'

When he didn't stop her Janey dared to reach out and rifle through the drawers of the desk. At the back of the overstuffed files she found what she was looking for. 'Fleet-feet,' she said, showing him the diagram. 'I'm wearing them. And this – Girl-gauntlet – that's my glove. I expect if we searched long enough we'd find sketches for all sorts of gadgets, and for the other Spylabs.'

'Spylabs?' Solomon gave a short laugh, struggling to stay composed. 'Laboratories for spies? This is all too much. You're winding me up!'

She had to prove it to him. There was no space overhead for a Fleet-feet jump so instead Janey dragged the picture of the Girl-gauntlet towards them. 'This looks like an old version,' she said, holding out her hand as she studied the diagram. 'Maybe even the first ever Gauntlet, as it looks so simple. But I've got stun gas, like it says here –' and she blasted a little puff of smoke away from their faces – 'and here where there used to be a pen, I've got a titanium blade.' Janey flicked out her tiny dagger blade, so small and yet so effective, and held it up for Solomon to study.

He examined it, a lopsided grin forming as he took it in. 'Amazing. And these . . . all this stuff,' he said, waving at all the diagrams and then touching the end of the blade carefully, 'was all invented by . . .'

And Janey smiled proudly. 'By you.'

The boy sniggered, half laughing, half questioning. 'But how do you know about all of this, Jane Blonde?'

'Because, in the future, you become my . . .' Careful, Janey, she thought, not wanting to freak him out completely. '. . . my boss. Solomon Brown. Head – no, creator – of Solomon's Polifical Investigations. Otherwise known as SPI.'

'I'm a spy,' said Solomon. 'A real spy?'

'Not just a spy.' Janey grinned at him. 'You're a super-SPI. Well, THE super-SPI, really.'

'I'm top dog.' Solomon nodded thoughtfully,

as though it was all starting to make sense. 'And you work for me.'

'And G-Mamma does, and the Halos, and loads of people. Mainly finding out what our arch-enemy, Copernicus, is up to, although at the moment that's nothing as he's safely behind glass at a NASA base.'

'So he causes all the problems, this . . . Copernicus.' Solomon rubbed his hand across his face. 'It's all a bit much to take in. Wow! But it all sort of . . . seems to fit. I always knew I was different, somehow.'

Special, thought Janey. He'd always known he was special. She smiled at the boy, who was now pacing in front of her, tugging at various pictures and then casting them aside. 'Would you like to see another of your Spylabs?' she said.

Solomon's eyes gleamed. 'Sure would,' he said, grinning. Then his face fell. 'Oh. I shouldn't really. We need to get back, now that I've found this –' he unpinned the picture of the R-Evolver, folded it carefully and stowed it away in his pocket – 'and now that I've found you, the girl from the rebus.'

'The what?'

'This.' From his other pocket Solomon pulled out the paper he'd been studying when she came in. It was a rough drawing of a girl with a high yellow ponytail, with 'JANE' written in the ponytail itself. Next to it was a sketch of a . . . Janey peered at it. What was that?

Two parallel lines, what looked like brackets either side of them, and two small ovals beneath them. She stood back a little and instantly the image became clear. A nose. Jane Blonde knows. The only other letter on it was a tiny B, and there was a small cross in the bottom right-hand corner.

'Why did you call it a rebus?'

'Cos that's what it is.' Solomon folded the paper and put it away. 'A puzzle with pictures for words. Our whole family loves them. And charades. All that rubbish.' He grinned sheepishly.

That reminded Janey of something. 'The other night you dropped something – a glass ball called a marble. And a note.'

'Oh. Sorry I wasn't able to stick around by the way – my first encounter with that machine didn't go as planned. That marble is actually – um, a gadget, I suppose we should call it now. It can see.' Solomon shook his head, amazed at his own brilliance. 'Well, it can take pictures. I've been getting photos of some boy's bedroom from it.'

Janey could barely contain her glee. She just managed to stop herself from shouting out, 'Oh, Dad!' 'There you are,' she said. 'Your first gadget. A single glass eye. You should give it a spy name.'

Solomon thought for a moment. 'How about . . . Spyclops? Like the one-eyed monster.'

'Perfect,' said Janey. She could hardly believe

it. Here she was with her father – at the very beginning of everything. 'And the note you dropped?'

Solomon's eyes grew sharp. 'Oh, yes. Did you work it out?'

'I didn't have time. Hang on.'

Grabbing a pen, Janey wrote out the strange word: EMOCME. 'It's almost like one of those words that's the same backwards as forwards.'

'Palindromes,' said Solomon, nodding.

'But it's not quite right – it doesn't work as one of those. It's . . .' Suddenly her puzzle focus switched on fully, and the answer sprang out at her from the page. 'It's a phrase.'

'And what does it say?' said Solomon eagerly, keen to hear that her logic was as honed as his.

Janey looked at it one more time and nodded. 'EMOC is C . . . O . . . M . . . E written backwards, plus the word ME. "Come back with me."'

Solomon laughed. 'You're right. Brilliant, Jane Blonde. You are absolutely right. And now we need to go.'

He looked very, very pleased with her. Janey grabbed his sleeve and pulled him along the corridor. If he was so thrilled at her working out a simple puzzle, imagine how delighted he was going to be when he saw all the other stuff she could do. Or rather, *they* could do, as a team.

They tumbled out of the clock, waiting for the swing

of both pendulums to reach the top simultaneously before shoving themselves through the space between, and closed the door carefully behind them.

'It's a secret place,' said Solomon. 'Always has been – and good to see it still is, here in the future. There's even a ghost story about it, to put people off looking. Nobody must ever know it's there.'

Janey nodded. 'I'm good at secrets,' she said. 'Like this, for instance.' She unstrapped her ASPIC from her leg and handed it to her boy-father. 'Aeronautical SPI Conveyor.'

'It's like one of those new skateboard contraptions,' said Solomon eagerly, turning it over in his hands. 'Where are the wheels?'

New? Janey wanted to laugh. Skateboards had been around as long as she could remember, but to her father in his boyish state they were the latest craze. 'No wheels,' she said. 'This one hovers. Just keep your feet evenly spread, and push on the back if you want to go up a wall.'

With the kind of excitement that Janey had only seen whenever Alfie got hold of some new fast form of transport, Solomon dropped the ASPIC and jumped on. She gave him a little shove in the back and he was off. 'What about yo— oh-oh-oh!'

Janey took to her Fleet-feet and pounded along next to him as he wobbled for the first hundred metres. He quickly got the hang of it, and whipped up the tall school gates and down the other side with barely a pause. At the end of the street he gave her a dazzling smile. 'Ace!' he called. And then he sped up.

'Da— Solomon! Wait for me!'

Even with her Fleet-feet at full stretch, Janey couldn't keep up. The boy spy was a natural on the ASPIC; she was pretty sure that when a skateboard came his way in his own time, he would quickly be able to impress everyone with his skills.

Minutes later she raced into the Spylab. Alfie was on his feet, knees bent, Boy-battler poised and ready to biff her into next week. 'Stop . . . You'll never . . .' Alfie saw Janey's face and dropped his hand. 'It's just you.'

At the same moment G-Mamma came pelting up the SPIral staircase. 'The Pet Jet hasn't been used since I was out there, Blondette,' she said, 'but I heard a scuffle kafuffle up here. What was going on, Baby Halo?'

'Some kid just came through the window on an ASPIC,' said Alfie with a shrug, 'and when I tried to stop him he grabbed the Satispy remote control and blasted off. I was just about to slug him as well,' he added with a guilty flush.

Janey slapped him on the back. 'Alfie, you are going to be so glad you didn't. Because you'll never guess who that was.'

The SPI:KE and boy Spylet listened, open-mouthed, as she described what had happened.

'So where's your dad gone now?' said Alfie in a hollow voice.

'I don't know!' Janey grinned. 'He's discovering all his gadgets – hasn't a clue how to work them yet though. We should go after him. *I* should go after him.'

G-Mamma looked up from the computer. 'Why you, Blondette?'

And for the first time in her joy at discovering the boy-Sol, Janey paused long enough to piece everything together.

'Because someone sent him to get me. And that someone is my dad – the older version! He's ended up stuck in the past and he's sent his younger self to make the journey here – giving him directions via a pictogram. Typical dad behaviour! For some reason he can't travel back himself, so he's counting on me to go back with young Sol and rescue him.'

It was her most important mission ever. And terrified as she was, she would not let him down.

Then Alfie cleared his throat. 'You'll need to find young Sol first.'

helter-skelter

'So your dad is really time-travelling?' shouted Alfie as they rushed along the SPI-Tube through space. 'Scary!'

Janey laughed. 'It can't be more scary than Satispying. Or this.' She stuck out her hand as the NASA sign loomed up to meet them; the rushing wind slowed long enough for them to hoist themselves out into the void where Copernicus's Spylab had once stood. The location bleeper on the Satispy remote had told them that Solomon was here.

'I don't know,' said Alfie, presenting his eyeball to a scanner beside the door. 'At least you know you exist here. When you travel back, you'll be going to a time before you were even thought of.'

Janey nodded. 'That's why I haven't told Sol who I really am. I thought it might do his head in.'

'Yeah, you do mine in all the time,' agreed Alfie with a cheeky sideways look.

'Shut up.'

'So why's he come here?' puffed Alfie. 'I thought he was in a hurry to take you back.'

'I told him about Copernicus – where he lives, and the problems he's caused. Perhaps Sol wants to deal with him while he can.'

'Clever.' Alfie skidded around a corner. 'Hope he manages it.'

They ran on. Doors hissed open as the retinal-recognition machinery verified their eyes. They slowed as they approached the closed-off space in which Copernicus hung. Janey held her breath for a moment, half expecting to find Solomon pressed up against the glass, or for Copernicus to be missing – escaped. But he was there, suspended in viscous goo that somehow kept him alive, his mutated organs still pumping. One huge yellow eye stared vacantly up towards the ceiling, as if searching for the sun, while the other was closed tight, just the occasional flicker of the eyelid giving any indication that the Squid Man was still alive.

Alfie hung back, pale. 'Well, there's my good old daddy,' he said with a sniff. 'Where's yours?'

Janey looked around. She had no idea, having assumed that Sol would head straight here. If he'd made it, of course – maybe his ever-increasing weakness from too many Satispy trips had started already, even now when he was barely a teenager. And for the first time Janey appreciated the danger that Alfie had spoken of. Messing with time *was* more dangerous, perhaps, than tampering with travel through space.

But it was a bit too late to be worrying about that. The clock near Copernicus's container showed the local time: 2200. 'What time is it by your watch, Alfie?'

Alfie was staring intently at his father, but he broke off to check his wristwatch. 'Three in the morning.'

'Then I don't want to worry you or anything, but it's like we've already time-travelled,' she said. 'Tube travel is so fast that we've landed yesterday, five hours before we set off.'

'Yuck,' said Alfie. 'No wonder I feel weird. Hey – look at that.' He shone the beam from his Boy-battler on to the glass cabinet.

Janey gasped. She hadn't spotted it because it was quite high up, but just on a level with the spooky yellow eye of the captive Copernicus a word was etched on to the glass.

EVƎ

'The second E's backwards,' said Alfie. 'What does that mean?'

'I don't know' But what was it her boy-father had said? '"Eve" is a palindrome,' she said excitedly. 'It reads the same backwards and forwards. Dad seemed to know all about them.'

Alfie nodded slowly. 'And written this way, it reads

exactly the same whichever side of the glass you're on.'

Janey stared at him. 'Like he was leaving The Big C a message or something.'

'Or Squid Man was leaving him one,' said Alfie with a shudder.

He was right. This was like a three-dimensional palindrome, the same backwards and forwards, from either side of the glass. And why did it look so familiar?

Before she could ponder on it any more, G-Mamma's voice blasted from her own and from Alfie's SPIVs simultaneously. 'Spylets! Get your little Lycra leggies back to base. Pronto!'

'What's up?' said Janey as she triggered the exit button and they sped back along the corridors.

'Sol just got back, shoved me out of the way, and ran out to the Pet Jet. He says he's going home!'

'Not without me he's not,' said Janey firmly. Jane Blonde was not going to let her father slip from under her nose again. 'Did he bring the Satispy control back?'

'Got it in my paw,' confirmed G-Mamma. 'Bringing you home now.'

Janey stepped forward beneath a skylight while Alfie dropped back. They had once Satispied together, to rather disastrous effect, so this time Janey was strictly on her own as her body dispersed into a solution of particles and streamed up to the Satispy satellite dish. With a groan, she felt her cells clang against the dish and zip back towards the Earth, and in moments she was gathering once more at G-Mamma's feet, which were clad in pink Turkish slippers to match her belly-dancing outfit.

'Bring Alfie back,' stammered Janey as soon as her jaw had reattached itself. 'I'm going after Sol.'

Janey ran at full tilt towards the back fence, slicing the gale-force wind with her dagger of a ponytail. The Pet Jet was balanced on one wing, the fat white tyre that housed the R-Evolver gyrating so fast it was little more than a blur. Through the middle glimmered a strange void, a darkness that was somehow blindingly bright . . .

'OK, Blonde – get this right,' Janey told herself sternly.

She sprang on to the top rail of the fence, thumped down hard with her feet and curved through the night sky like a rainbow of silver, diving head first into the dark-light. Heading for what, she didn't know. As the R-Evolver opened its mouth to swallow her up, she could only wish that some time soon it would spit her out again.

'No! Help!'

She found herself careering at breakneck speed down an enormous helter-skelter, face first, her arms trapped beneath her, the velocity so extreme that her head was pushed against her neck, almost to breaking point. It was impossible to turn around. To slow down. To stop.

Faster and faster she slid, only just able to turn her head enough to see through the clear spiralling water-slide-like tube she was in. An identical helter-skelter ran off to one side into the dizzying depths beneath her. Every so often she would pass an opening off the slide, with a similar, shorter helter-skelter leading off it, but without being able to reach out a hand to slow herself there was no way to get a good look. The SPIV dug painfully into her chest . . . her cheeks were practically wrapped around her ears, the G-force was so riotous . . . She felt very, very sick, and there was no sign of this ride ever ending . . .

But suddenly a face appeared below Janey. It was racing towards her. No – *she* was racing towards it! Any second now they'd collide. Her head would be knocked off! But just as impact became inevitable the face was replaced by a hand, which reached out and grabbed the only thing it could – the end of her Blonde ponytail. Janey tried to scream but the speed she was travelling down the Time Slide ripped away the sound. She imagined hearing the snap of her neck as her head was pulled to one side. But the hand had let go now and Janey was rocketing head first again, down a shorter spiralling slide, nose almost pressed against someone's muddy shoes.

They shot out, one after the other, narrowly avoiding collision as their bodies somersaulted and bucked through the air before landing with no cushioning whatsoever on a grassy bank. Janey lay there, winded and confused.

'You're supposed to programme it, you dork,' said a voice coming from somewhere over her head. 'I thought you knew everything. Jane Blonde, the one who knows . . . hmmm.'

Janey shook herself and sat up gingerly. Apart from her screaming scalp, nothing seemed damaged. 'Well, I don't know how to do that,' she said.

'You'd better learn then, like I did.' Solomon held out a hand to help her to her feet.

'Why did you run off?'

'Oh.' Solomon looked distinctly uncomfortable. 'That monster thing scared me. I swear it saw me, and then its snaky-arm tentacle floated up through the water and scratched on the glass. I know – I'm mad.'

Janey gasped. 'No! There *was* a word on there: EVƎ. Copernicus must have been trying to send us a message.'

'Disgusting,' said Solomon with a gulp.

And worrying. Copernicus could cause a huge amount of trouble. It was even more important that she find her dad – her grown-up dad – as quickly as possible. She looked around. 'So where am I?'

'It's not so much *where*,' grinned the boy who was her father, 'as *when*. Jane Blonde, you're in my time now.'

6 cellar fella

'Cool!' Janey hurried to catch up with her boy-father. They had popped out of a tyre attached to a tractor in a vast, boggy field, and now he was striding towards the gate. 'But really – where in your time?'

'Home,' said Solomon, leaping the gate nimbly and pulling a bike out from the hedge. 'Which I think is your area before they built all those new houses.'

He handed her the ASPIC as Janey looked around, taking in the fields and distant neighs and squawks of farm animals. In the distance she could see the church spire in Winton town centre. In her own time the same area would be teeming with life.

'Now – keep up with the chopper if you can.'

The chopper? As Sol pedalled off, Janey wanted to laugh at the nickname he'd given himself – until she realized he meant his bike, with its long handlebars. Before she lost sight of him, she dropped the ASPIC to the ground and bounced off across the field.

'I can't believe it!' she shouted as she caught him up, the moonlight glinting off the ASPIC. 'Isn't this where Winton School should be?'

'Winton? No, the only school around here is Everdene.'

Solomon spun the pedals faster, but Janey hung back a little, sure she was right. 'Help me out, Gogs,' she whispered. Her Ultra-gogs rattled into life and overlaid a diagram of buildings in Janey's time on to the landscape before her. She was right; over to the left was where the football pitch would be. In the distance should have been Solfari Lands, but there were simply large expanses of grass where the Spylab and the Amphibian House and all the rest of the zoo would be. Of course, she thought after a moment. Both the school and the zoo were her father's creations. He just hadn't got round to them yet.

There was one place, however, that did exist in both their times, and Solomon was soft-pedalling to a halt in front of it. The Hallidays' house. Without the school, it was just a big stone house sitting in a great expanse of land, with rather beautiful landscaped gardens rolling away as far as she could see. Janey gasped. 'This place looks amazing,' she said. 'That view's incredible!'

Solomon put a finger to his lips and beckoned her around the back of the house. 'Just stupid gardens,' he muttered with a frown. 'Always getting people mooching around them, asking about the ancestors.'

'Ancestors?'

'Capability Brown – the landscape architect. Anyway, quietly does it – don't want the parents to hear us, nosy old codgers.'

Janey followed him through the cellar door, perplexed. What were they doing here? And Capability Brown – that name did sound familiar; she was pretty sure that G-Mamma had told her that her father was descended from him, but hadn't she also said Jane Blonde came from a long line of spies? Planting petunias didn't sound very spy-like.

Solomon pointed at the ceiling as it creaked with the tell-tale sounds of someone pacing the floor above them.

'Mum and Dad must be up,' he hissed, alarmed. 'Thought I'd managed to escape while they were asleep.'

A muffled voice floated down through the exposed floorboards. Solomon strained to hear what was being said, then sighed when he found it was impossible.

Janey grinned, then fished in her pocket for her SPI-Pod. Handing one of the earphones to the boy, she scampered up a nearby ladder and pressed the listening device to the ceiling. Solomon followed her lead, puzzled, then stared with wide eyes when voices boomed into their ears.

'. . . bit out of control,' a deep male voice was saying.

43

'But that doesn't help us,' a female replied. Janey couldn't believe that her very own grandparents, whom she'd never met, were talking right above her head. 'Our son is sick, Lancelot.'

Sick? Janey looked sideways at Solomon, but he just rolled his eyes in a way that suggested they were always going on like that and pushed his earphone in a bit further. He did look a bit ill, she thought. His forehead was slick with sweat and his breathing a little wheezy. 'Are you OK?' she mouthed.

He nodded, making swirly motions with his finger. The R-Evolver slide – that was what was making him feel nauseous.

'. . . when he gets home. Have to lock his door,' Janey's grandfather said firmly.

'Oh, Lancelot.' Her grandmother sighed. 'That's not necessary, surely?'

The male voice waxed and waned as Solomon's father criss-crossed the room. '. . . told you, Carmel . . . control . . . danger . . . to be safe than sorry.'

A flash of anger crossed Solomon's face, and Janey hurried down the ladder, past the pots of paint and old bike parts, and pulled the earphone from his ear. He stared at her for a moment, and then his shoulders slumped.

'Peasants,' he hissed, pointing upwards.

'They're just worried about you,' she whispered back.

He nodded, staring at her as if he'd forgotten she was there. 'I suppose so. I'd better go and face the music. Wait here until I get you. I'll go and have a word with er, someone, and we'll work out what to do next.'

'OK.' But Janey was desperate to follow him. *Someone* – he must mean her father (although it sounded like he didn't know it yet). She could understand why older Sol would have kept young Sol a touch in the dark about his true identity. 'Can I come? Please!'

'Not yet. We'll wait until the coast is clear.'

'Oh.' Janey's disappointment ran deep. She'd been so sure she was going to see her dad as soon as she arrived in the past. 'If you think so.'

'It's for the best.'

Young Solomon left the cellar, pausing for a moment at the threshold to nod seriously at Janey before slipping out of the door and bolting it after him. 'Don't want her snooping around and upsetting the wrinklies. Bad enough as it is,' he muttered, not realizing that Janey's SPI-Pod earpiece still dangled and she could hear every word.

For a second Janey panicked, but then she checked herself. She could understand. Her grandparents definitely sounded twitchy, and he had to make it look exactly as it had before so nobody would suspect she was there.

She waited for voices in the kitchen, but

whatever discussion there was took place further down the hall, and even her SPI-Pod didn't allow for enhanced hearing at that distance. Wishing she had Trouble with her to keep her warm, Janey snuggled down behind a teetering mound of flowerpots and waited for her father to release her.

The scrape of a kitchen chair above her woke her up. Janey gasped as she peered around the gloomy cellar. What time was it? As she tried to gather her thoughts, her father's boyish voice muttered something upstairs, then shouted 'No!' She couldn't make out the words of her grandmother's calm reply. Then footsteps tracked across the floor.

Janey struggled stiffly from her plant-pot bed and brushed herself down as the front door banged. Any moment now her father would release the bolts and free her, and she wanted to look alert. Twiddling her SPI-Pod, Janey listened to her father tramp around the side of the house. He was at the back door. She shuffled forward. But then she heard the unmistakable slam of a car door – two – followed by the grind of tyres on gravel. 'X-ray!' she cried to her Ultra-gogs.

They focused on the cellar wall so that Janey's vision could penetrate to the scene beyond. Her father, looking very truculent, was being driven away by the shadowy figure of her grandfather. Solomon stared at the door he had locked behind him, and for a moment Janey wondered if he knew she could see him.

Surely he'd come back for her.

Hours later Janey realized he was not coming back. She was stuck in a grimy cellar, in a different era to the one she was meant to be in. What time would it be at home? Was she meant to be off to school herself? Her mother would probably be frantic with worry.

Then the car finally came back, and Janey's hopes soared only to be dashed. It had only one passenger – Lancelot Brown. He trod heavily across the gravel around to the front door. Where was Solomon? Very crossly Janey pushed on the cellar door. It didn't even judder under a frantic thump from her Girl-gauntlet, and she didn't dare try again for fear of giving her location away. She X-rayed the door. It was very firmly bolted, top and bottom. Nothing less than a blast of SPInamite was going to get it off its hinges and out of her way.

Another car. Upstairs in the house there was a knock at the door. 'It's the doctor, Carmel,' called Lancelot Brown from the front of the house, and Janey listened as her grandmother's light footsteps tapped away down the hall. Now was her chance. Even so, she hesitated. If she blew up the cellar door, her father would get the blame and be in even more trouble.

Janey looked around quickly. She would blow through the wall – it was stone and would probably suffer less damage than a heavy wooden door, but hopefully there would be a big enough hole for Janey to squeeze through. Whipping her SPInamite from a concealed pocket on her SPIsuit sleeve, Janey chewed desperately for a few seconds, wedged the sticky mass into the angle between the bottom brick and the floor, and took cover behind the paint pots.

Whumffff. The SPInamite detonated with a dull crump, and Janey rushed over just in time to stop the column of earthenware flower pots clattering to the ground. As she carefully stood them back on end she studied the hole she'd made, which had actually gone through the floor rather than the wall.

She dropped to her knees and laughed. Her father had already been hard at work in the cellar, planning his Spylabs even at his current young age. Leading from the jagged hole was the outline of what was definitely a tunnel.

Without hesitation, Janey pulled a tarpaulin across behind her, dropped into the hole on top of her ASPIC and covered her tracks with the cloth. Then, 'Light,' she instructed her Ultra-gogs, and she took off along the tunnel. She had to crouch double, but she was still able to zoom along like a very lithe little mole.

After a few minutes and several miles, the Ultra-gogs bleeped. A door. There was no immediate sound from the other side so Janey pushed it open.

It hardly surprised her at all when she stepped

out into her father's den under the stage, with just a few drawings littering the makeshift desk, along with a cloth sack of marbles and a sketch pad covered in what looked like noughts-and-crosses grids. Janey grinned as she peered closer. They were early codes.

T E N

E V E

N E T

A N D

N A N

D N A

'Palindromes!' said Janey, reading the sentences back-wards and forwards. The little grids were palindrome squares or something. 'That's my dad!'

She was still smiling to herself as she picked her way carefully out of the clock into the Everdene entrance hall, checking the face as she closed the door behind her. It was ten o'clock, and something was happening in the school hall. Fortunately there was nobody around to see her in her strange silver outfit, but, just to be sure, Janey scuttled in through the door and hid in the long velvet curtains alongside the stage.

A tall, vigorous girl was marching around the hall with a clipboard. She looked incredibly at home, and also familiar. She called out, 'Jakobi, could you line the tables up down the middle of the hall, leading from the stage. It's a catwalk, for goodness sake, not an obstacle course. The models should be able to just walk off the stage, not have to leap like gazelles. Jakobi!'

'I'm just checking some . . .' The boy she was instructing stood back and studied the stage, hands on hips, blue eyes peeping out from behind an outrageously long sandy fringe. He flicked it out of the way self-consciously as he scanned the area and focused for a second on the curtains behind which she hid. Jakobi. Head Boy, opposite number to the tall girl who now stalked up to him and swiped him across the head with her clipboard.

'*I'm* on checking,' she snapped. 'You're on doing.'

Janey squeaked with glee as she spied the Head Girl badge pinned to the girl's chest. Alfie's mum! Looked like her future as a headmistress was already marked out for her.

She shouldn't have laughed aloud. Suddenly the curtain she was hiding in twitched, and Janey whipped round, alarmed.

A girl her own age was glaring at her with round china-blue eyes that were doubled in size by her thick glasses. On either side of the chubby face hung a fat brown plait, and the generous mouth was furiously chewing gum. 'What are you doing?' hissed the girl to Janey. 'Oh lord. You're st-st-stealing my designs, aren't you? Oh please don't! Oh lordy lord.'

Janey's mouth fell open. 'You're . . . G-Ma . . . G-Mamm . . .'

'Rosie!' hollered Maisie Halliday from the hall as Janey and her future SPI:KE stared at each other in horror. 'Rosie Biggenham, where are you?'

And the roly-poly girl tried to pull the curtain aside. 'There's a sp-spy in the camp,' she said, pointing at Janey, just at the same moment as her foot came free of the curtain fabric and she fell face first, straight off the stage.

a passion for fashion

Janey couldn't help herself. 'G-Mamma!' she called, and leaped down out of the curtains to help her young SPI:KE-to-be up off the floor. The girl flailed around, trying to hide her sketch pad, find her feet and talk to Maisie Halliday all at the same time.

'She's st-st-stealing our ideas! Look at her c-clothes,' she shouted to the Head Girl, her big eyes squeezing shut each time she stuttered. 'And she's c-c-calling me something weird . . . Gee-m-m-m . . .'

Maisie peered at Janey suspiciously. 'Well, that is a very strange get-up you're wearing. Who are you? And this Gee-ma person you're looking for – do you mean Geneva?'

Time to think fast, Blonde, Janey told herself. 'No, I was just shouting, um, Geronimo! When she fell off the stage.'

'So what were you doing in the curtains? You're from the stage school in Bowood, aren't you? You lot

52

are always trying to steal our ideas.' Maisie gave her
another once-over and sniffed. Even as a teenager, she
was scary and stern.

Janey looked down at her SPIsuit. It did look
strange next to the bottle-green uniform both the other
girls were wearing. 'No, no, I'm just new to Everdene,'
she said quickly, 'and I don't have my uniform yet.
This is my . . . sports gear.'

Maisie and the awe-struck Rosie Biggenham
gawped at her. Then Maisie shook her head. 'You look
like an Olympic gymnast, for goodness sake,' she said
scathingly. 'You need blue shorts and a green Aertex top
for Phys. Ed. You can get them from the school office.
Now, Rosie,' she said briskly, turning her attention to
the other girl, whose hair was escaping from her plaits
and standing out in a frizzy halo around her face. 'We
have twenty minutes. Pin down that compère of yours
now, or find a replacement.'

As Maisie stalked away, directing two sweating
boys to prop several vast mirrors up on the stage, the
future G-Mamma turned very pink. 'Oh lordy lordy
lordy lordy lordy. Where did K-K-Kobi go?'

Janey followed Rosie back on to the stage behind
the curtains, where she started frantically rifling through
a pile of clothes as if Kobi might be hidden in there.
'Who's Kobi?'

'The Head Boy. He's s-s-supposed to be the
compère. Where's he got to?' Rosie looked close

to tears. 'He's got this b-b-b-big voice that goes right to the back of the hall.'

And so have you in my world, thought Janey, hardly able to connect this stammering, bumbling girl with her vivacious SPI:KE. The girl was now on her knees, wailing mournfully as she pulled outfits together from the pile. 'Great clothes,' said Janey. That was more like it – big flared trousers and flowing tops and dresses in geometric shapes and vibrant colours. 'Did you make these?'

Rosie nodded. 'All of them. It's taken me weeks and weeks. B-b-but it's all going to be p-p-pointless.'

A gaggle of girls and a couple of boys trooped up the stairs, and Rosie handed them their outfits one by one. 'Anne, th-th-that's yours; Robert, the g-g-green one, p-p-p . . .'

'Please!' finished Robert rudely, grabbing the outfit from Rosie's shaking fingers.

Rosie winced, her eyes squeezing shut again. She's even more reserved and nervy than I used to be, thought Janey. The last girl rushed past, all long legs and coppery hair, peeling off her school jumper as she went by. 'Kobi's gone home ill, Rosie,' she said, her voice muffled by the silken shirt that was now over her head. 'Sick of Maisie, most likely.'

At that, Rosie Biggenham turned completely white, her blue eyes fluttering shut. 'But he's the . . . the . . . the . . .'

'Rosie,' said Janey, giving the girl's shoulders a shake, 'don't faint!'

'Five minutes,' hissed Maisie Halliday from the side of the stage. 'Rosie, the school's filing in. Speed it up!'

'I can't! I c-c-c-can't do it on my own.' Rosie held up the one remaining outfit, a pair of purple trousers, a vast black pirate's shirt and a curly black wig like Captain Hook might wear. 'Kobi was going to wear this . . . do the t-t-talking . . . it's all useless . . .'

She was falling apart. Janey wondered whether she was going to have to give her SPI:KE of the future a slap across the face, just to calm her down. The lights in the hall were dimming as a look of sheer terror fixed itself on to Rosie's face. The models were all staring at her, waiting for the show to start, waiting for Rosie to take charge. The copper-haired girl was chewing her lip, almost as anxious as Rosie. Or rather, Janey realized, anxious *for* Rosie. The expression of concern was one she was sure she'd seen somewhere before . . .

Peeking through the curtains, Janey could see that the hall had filled up completely, and all eyes were on the stage. There was an awful feeling of expectancy in the room, and Janey struggled to work out what it was.

Then it came to her. They were expecting Rosie to blow it. Her future SPI:KE was about to become a laughing stock in front of the whole school.

And suddenly Janey burst into action.

'Oh no you don't,' she hissed fiercely towards the body of the hall. She grabbed the black shirt, shoved it over Rosie Biggenham's head, and tied the purple trousers round her middle like a piratical sash. The black curly wig finished off the outfit, and Janey grinned as she removed the thick glasses from Rosie's astonished face.

'Wear these,' she said, replacing them with her Ultra-gogs. 'Say "running order" and they'll tell you which outfit's coming next. Go on,' she said, giving Rosie a shove. 'You can do it.'

'How do you know?' squeaked Rosie.

She already looked several inches taller, Janey noticed, and it wasn't just the height of the curls in the wig. 'Trust me,' she said. 'You're amazing.'

Rosie stumbled to the middle of the stage, stuttering, 'Oh lordy, lordy, lordy Lord,' and facing the back as she faltered to a halt. 'I can't I can't I can't I can't I . . .'

There was a horrible, air-sucking pause and Janey waited with the rest of the audience for the girl to burst into tears, run off the stage, spontaneously combust . . .

But then Rosie's head came up. She saw herself in the mirrors behind the catwalk, and the copper-haired girl giving her an enormous thumbs-up backstage. As she took in her dramatic appearance, a smile spread slowly over Rosie's face, then her right hip dropped in time with the beat. With a wicked grin at Janey, she spun around to face the audience.

And G-Mamma was born.

'Boys and girls . . .' she shouted, lifting her arms above her head in a victorious and glorious V, 'teachers divine . . . ladles and jellyspoons . . . it's catwalk time!'

'What? That wasn't in the script,' muttered Maisie, as she leafed through the sheets on her clipboard. 'Who is that, anyway?'

The lights flared, the music pounded with some song about a dandy highwayman, which was exactly what Rosie looked like, and the model with the copper-tinted hair launched herself down the catwalk to the cries and applause of the delighted crowd. 'Geneva, ladies and gentlemen, wearing "Divine Disco Diva!"' shouted the new improved Rosie Biggenham, and Janey huddled in the curtains, laughing with delight as her SPI-Pod volleyed snippets of conversation from the audience: 'Who *is* that? Rosie Biggenham? No way! She's amazing! Yeah, she looks gorgeous!'

Model after model coursed down the catwalk, with Rosie word-perfect on each name and outfit. The Ultra-gogs, besides looking fantastic, were doing a very good job with the running order.

Geneva ran past Janey, laughing. 'Isn't she brilliant?'

'Sure is.' Then Janey stared at Geneva. 'What . . . what's your name again?'

The girl grinned, and Janey's heart turned over. 'Geneva. Sometimes Gene or Genie. You're new, aren't you? What's your name?'

'Jane, um, Blondette,' said Janey quickly.

'Oh, that sounds French or something. I'm half Swiss – that's why I'm called Geneva. Maybe you come from somewhere near me?'

Geneva had looked away and was nodding to the beat. Very near you, thought Janey, the tingling across her nose warning her she might cry. So near you wouldn't believe. She wondered how the extravagantly beautiful Geneva had ended up settling for an existence as plain old Jean Brown.

A million questions spilled into her brain, but most of all she just wanted to hug this girl who would become her mother. Geneva had already walked away though – just as well really, Janey realized. She'd think it very odd to be grabbed by a stranger in a silver suit. Rosie scooted over to her as applause rang out around the room, along with chants of: 'RO-SIE, RO-SIE, RO-SIE . . .'

'Listen to that!' Rosie grabbed Janey's hands. 'They LOVE me! And I'm not stammering . . . and I look outstanding . . . and these glasses, they're just fantastic. I have got to get me some of these. How did you do it? How did you t-t-transform me?'

Like you'll transform me one day, Janey wanted to say – when you let me be someone else for a while.

58

Someone special. 'It's a secret,' she said. 'But really you did it yourself. And listen –' She cocked her head towards the school hall. 'They're calling for you.'

'Ro-sie B! Ro-sie B! Ro-sie B!' The girl in the curly wig nodded along, her smile getting broader and broader. 'Ro-sie B! That's – so – me! Hey, I keep rhyming without meaning to.'

'You're good at that,' replied Janey. 'You'd better go.'

'Wait right here,' said Rosie sternly, waving to her models and sauntering cheekily down the catwalk.

Janey wanted to watch forever. But it wasn't until she was told to stay put by the girl who would become her SPI:Kid Educator that Janey remembered why she was there in the first place. The grown-up G-Mamma would be waiting for her somewhere. Not to mention the grown-up Geneva. And her father.

As for young Sol, he was definitely out of the limelight. She spotted him in the background, operating the lights on Maisie's instructions. He kept looking around anxiously, but Maisie snapped at him, 'Don't think you're rushing off, Brown. You were two hours late, so you can stay to the end of the clearing up.'

'Sorry. I had a . . . doctor's appointment.'

So that was what had gone wrong with the plan. He'd been unexpectedly dragged away by his father that morning. And there was no way now that Maisie was going to let him out of her sight . . . Janey sighed. She thought she might as well go and wait for him at his house, where they could talk in private. And she had a sudden urge to check out her grandparents again . . .

She took advantage of the melee and slipped out of the hall. The whole school was involved in the fashion show. Even though the bell was ringing for lunchtime, many of them still thronged on the stage and around the grandfather clock, making access to the underground tunnel impossible. Still, it was easy to trot down the corridor and out of the main school doors, then Fleet-feet across country, back to the school house. Or rather, to the Browns' house, as it was right now.

Even with her Fleet-feet it took twenty minutes to get back to the house. At the gateway to the house she hesitated. She'd never met any of her grandparents as they'd all died before she was born. But just beyond the thick oak door were two important, beloved family members. It was too much to resist.

Flitting through the garden, Janey made her way to the side of the house and turned up her SPI-Pod. There they were, in the lounge. She crouched down under the window, just in time to hear her grandfather say, '. . . on the pillowcase?'

A flapping noise. Her grandmother was obviously holding something up. 'A picture of a girl and a . . . nose? And then this word under a drawing of the tractor, I think. BELIEVE.'

'And Solomon's denying all knowledge of it? You have to admit it's a worry, Carmel. He's getting more and more withdrawn – and disappearing like that for hours on end! He's a law unto himself.'

'But you can't believe Solomon had anything to do with the illness,' said Carmel Brown, as if she didn't want to believe it herself.

'I don't know.' Lancelot sighed. 'It defies logic, of course . . .'

Janey's grandmother laughed. 'When has this family ever worried about that. You just need to . . . oh, there you are, darling."

They'd been interrupted. Janey instinctively went to instruct her Ultra-gogs to X-ray through the wall, but then she remembered that Rosie was still wearing them. As quietly as possible, Janey lifted her nose above the window sill, just as her grandmother said, 'No, darling, back to bed. Best place for you. I'll come and sit with you.'

A figure in pale blue pyjamas with dark blue trim turned away from the door. Janey dropped down to the floor again. Her father had managed to get back from school ahead of her! And was he really ill? She sighed with exasperation. If they kept hanging about and looking after him, she'd never get him on his own. How was she supposed to find her adult father without the help of his younger self? He could be anywhere!

Then a delicious thought occurred to her. If she went forward in time again, she could perhaps come back at the moment before they'd gone into the cellar. Then she could warn young Sol to prevent his parents from carting him off in the car again. Of course! They could manage the whole situation differently, and she could get straight to the mission at hand and rescue her father.

Time to go, thought Janey, and she scurried through the garden, Fleet-feet jumped the fence and sped out to the field with the tractor. Just in time she remembered what her boy-father had explained: the R-Evolver needed programming somehow.

There was nothing at all on the outside of the machine that indicated what to do. So Janey took a deep breath and stuck her hand into the shaft of blackness. Immediately blinding light burst through the gash she had created, splitting into little blobs like spilled mercury. To Janey's astonishment, the silvery globules gathered in formation against the column of darkness, forming what looked like a row of thousands of elevator buttons. With a name hanging above them.

BELIEVᴲ.

She remembered her grandmother's words. *'And then this word under a drawing of the tractor, I think. BELIEVE.'*

So the time helter-skelter inside the R-Evolver

was the BELIEVƎ machine – and that's what the second part of Sol's rebus had referred to. *Use the BELIEVE machine to find Jane Blonde. The one who knows.* And it was easy to see how young Solomon had found her. She peered more closely at the row of buttons. Each was accompanied by a holographic revolving head and a woman's name. Janey started with the one on the far left. THE MIGHTY EVE. She didn't look particularly mighty, just hairy, but there was a wisdom in her eyes that made Janey's neck tingle.

She ran her finger along the line until suddenly, almost as she reached the far end, she spotted a name she recognized, beneath the image of a woman with clear eyes and a slender nose: Monique the Unique Delacroix. The surname was the same as Jakobi's, the disappearing Head Boy. Perhaps this stunning, intelligent woman with rich red curls and the exotic name was related to him. Then she gasped. Next to Monique was a face (and a beautiful helmet of copper hair) that she definitely knew. Gina Bellarina. And then, finally, the most recognizable name and face of all. The last on the panel.

A girl with a platinum ponytail.

Jane Blonde.

Janey shivered and the faces blurred. MIGHTY EVE. Monique the Unique. Her mother. Herself. The unknown heads. All she wanted now was

63

to get home, to see G-Mamma, and – most definitely – to ask her mum some questions.

As the silvery images wavered before her eyes Janey took a deep breath, pushed the mercury-light button beside her own name and jumped into the R-Evolver. On to the BELIEVƎ helter-skelter. The centre of time. And all she had to do to use it, to travel through time, was hold on to her dreams, her memories, and take a chance. *Believe* she could make a difference. *Believe* she could help her father – her whole family. *Believe*, in the end, in herself.

Helter-skeltering upwards was pretty vomit-making, and soon Janey stopped trying to think and just concentrated on hanging on to her insides. But before very long she corkscrewed out of the Pet Jet tyre and toppled on to the grass in her very own garden. Jane Blonde time. She lay there for a moment, trying to catch her breath, as the back door of the house opened.

'A day and a half!' Her mother sounded frantic. 'I've been worried sick. You've got some explaining to do, missy . . .'

But before Jean could say another word, G-Mamma shouted, 'Look out! The R-Evolver . . . !'

It was too late. The large object shot out of the BELIEVƎ centre like a squishy bullet, landing right on top of Janey in a tangle of black silk shirt and glossy jet curls.

Rosie Biggenham stared down at Janey through the Ultra-gogs. 'These specs are very, very clever,' she said breathlessly, then she struggled to her feet as two grown women, who no doubt looked very oddly familiar, ran across the grass towards them.

8 rosie and the g

They sat around the little square table in Janey's kitchen, the very same place in which G-Mamma had first told Janey of her Spylet future. Now they were using the same location to explain to G-Mamma about *her* spy future. Her SPI:KE future, in fact.

G-Mamma eyed her young self with a slightly sickened expression. 'I wish you'd take that wig off. I look much better blonde.'

Rosie stared back, then slowly removed the wig. G-Mamma contemplated the frizzy brown plaits for a long moment, then said, 'Actually . . . put it back on.'

'S-s-so you're telling me,' said Rosie, nervousness bringing her stutter back, 'that this is the future, and you're all spies, and I turn into –' and she pointed a shaking finger at the woman in the clown outfit across the table – 'you: G-Ma-Ma-Ma-Mam-ma.'

G-Mamma rolled her eyes, crimson bursts appearing on each cheek. 'Oh, stop it! I have not stammered since that fa-fa-fa-fa . . . You say it!' she barked at Janey.

'Fashion show,' said Janey quietly. She was watching her mother carefully, but Jean was simply sitting very quietly, with her hands in her lap, looking from Rosie to G-Mamma with a scrutiny bordering on rudeness.

Suddenly Jean smacked the table. 'That's right! That fashion show, where you suddenly wowed everyone with your new appearance, this new flamboyant personality. And you looked like . . . like that.'

Now Jean stared at Rosie once more, and Rosie stared back. 'Hang on,' said the girl. 'Don't tell me you were at that fashion show too. Who are you, anyway?'

This should be interesting, thought Janey. Her mother paused for a moment, then said, 'Rosie, I don't want to completely blow your mind apart with information until I've spoken more fully to my daughter.'

'And th-that's you?' Rosie peered at Janey through the Ultra-gogs.

'Yes. Hey – that's how you followed me, isn't it? You used Track and Trace on the Gogs . . . I mean, glasses.'

'The specs? Yeah,' said Rosie with a nod. 'They led me right out the back of the B-B-Browns' garden and up this swivelly tube.'

'Can I have them back?'

'No.' Rosie looked quite sulky. 'They make me c-c-c-cool.'

'Not with that stammer. Lordy lord lordy,' groaned G-Mamma.

'I say that too,' said Rosie, perplexed.

'Of course you do, fool! You are me! What they teaching at school? One and one makes three? Oh, that rhymed.'

'I rhyme.' Rosie's eyes bulged. 'I rhyme all the time.'

'It's not a crime. Hah! Can't stop the rhyme.'

And the two G-Mammas, young and not so young, eyeballed each other across the table and then started following each other in some strange body-popping moves, first one then the other, in a competition across time.

Jean Brown leaned across to Janey. 'So, now that they're occupied, perhaps you could tell me what on earth's going on.'

'Well . . . a few days ago Dad appeared, only as a boy, and he showed me the secret den where he first started inventing things.' Janey grinned excitedly. 'It's where he actually began being a spy! And then he wanted me to go back with him, so we went in this helter-skelter in the R-Evolver called BELIEVE, only the second E's backwards, and I went back to his house and then to Everdene and there was the fashion show and . . .'

They talked on and on, and Janey got all the reac-

tions she'd expected and tried to avoid. Astonishment.
Anger when Jean learned what risks Janey had taken.
And then disappointment, a disappointment that had
stung horribly, when Janey revealed that she still hadn't,
in fact, seen her grown-up father, despite everything.
At this, Jean Brown left the room for a minute or two,
then came out of the bathroom blowing her nose and
saying she must have hay fever, but Janey knew the
truth. Her mother's heart had just broken a little bit
more. It made Janey all the more determined, if that
was possible, to fix things. Fix everything.

Suddenly her mother frowned. 'So – did you meet
me?'

Janey grinned. 'I met Geneva.'

Her mother's eyes grew hazy. 'Gina for short.
Geneva "Gina" Delacroix.'

'Delacroix?' Janey swivelled around, excited. She
remembered the elevator button. 'Don't tell me that
was your maiden name! The same as . . . Monique the
Unique!'

'My mum,' said her mother, smiling. 'She died
when I was little. I was brought up by her parents, so I
used her name. And then when I started spying, your
father crossed it with "ballerina" – I was a good dancer,
you know – and Geneva Delacroix became Gina
Bellarina.' For a moment Janey's mother became lost in
her memories, but then she shook herself. 'Who told
you about Monique? Someone in the past?'

69

Janey explained the centre of the R-Evolver and the line of heads and names that included both herself and her mother and, it now turned out, her mother's mother. 'Why don't you come back with me? I can show you!'

'Maybe later. I need you to go to NASA for me now,' said Jean. 'Your news about Copernicus scratching messages inside his case concerns me; he might not be as harmless there as we think. You know him best. You should check.'

'I'll take Alfie,' said Janey, thinking of the last time they'd been there. 'He saw what state he was in too. He'll know if there's been any change.'

Jean pointed to G-Mamma and Rosie, who were now rolling grapes across the table into each other's open mouths, seeing who could fit most in without choking. 'I'll rally the other SPIs and try to keep these two focused, while you and Halo head off to NASA. Then we can get back to tracking down your father.'

Less than an hour later Jane Blonde and Al Halo were whizzing their way back to Florida. In as little time as she could, Janey explained what had been going on.

'So you thought it was me, but it was actually your dad as a boy, and he used to live in my house? Weird!' Alfie flashed past the retinal-recognition system with Janey in hot pursuit.

'Slow down! What are you rushing for?'

They skidded to a stop in front of Copernicus's case. 'I want to get back to see this young G-Mamma before they send her home again. That's got to be a laugh.' He stared up at the half-squid behind the glass. 'Euw.'

'Oh, he looks terrible!' Janey almost felt sorry for their arch-enemy. His slimy skin was almost transparent, blue veins standing out like roads on a map all over his face and body, and horrible red threads like a spider's web across his staring yellow eye. 'I don't think he'll last much longer.'

'What a shame,' said Alfie sarcastically. 'Righto. Well, he's not a danger to anyone in this state. Let's get back and tell your mum he's about to croak.'

'Alfie,' said Janey gently, 'that is your dad, you know. It's all right to care a bit about him.'

'Says who?' Alfie grinned at her in a slightly mad, over-bright fashion and sped back along the corridor.

With a sigh Janey ASPIC'd after him. Families were so complicated.

On their return to the Spylab they were amazed to find G-Mamma lying on one of the benches with Trouble on her stomach, purring at intervals, as Rosie ran around the lab carrying out her orders.

Alfie watched Rosie with open-mouthed amazement. 'Apart from the SPI-buys, she looks so . . . so *normal*.'

Now that she'd removed the wig, Rosie did look like a normal schoolgirl, apart from the fact that gadgets of every variety were trailing from her body. She pushed the orange PERSPIRE back on her head to wipe the sweat from her forehead as G-Mamma shouted, 'Back-boat! You never know when you might need one of those. There's definitely a time at Guide camp in about two years where that will come in VERY handy.'

'So . . . Back-boat for Girl Guides, and wotcha-macallit for the oojimaflop, and SPI-Pod for getting the answers from you in the future at the Interschools Quiz, and Ultra-gogs to X-ray the girl's toilets and avoid Burly Brenda sticking my head down the loo, and . . . and . . .' Rosie paused, staring at her shoes. 'What are the s-s-secret feet for?'

'Fleet-feet,' said G-Mamma hoarsely, moving Trouble off her chest. 'Gymnastics in Phys. Ed., term three. You will vault that horse like a pro, and you will not, repeat NOT, end up sprawled on the top with your big behind splitting your shorts and making you the laughing stock of the class. Make that the school. No, make that the whole town!'

With Alfie looking a bit ill at the vision G-Mamma had just painted in his head, Janey intercepted the large golden ASPIC her SPI:KE had been about to hand to Rosie. 'G-Mamma, you can't go giving yourself SPI-buys to get you out of trouble in the past. You'll cause some dreadful time-twist thing.'

'It'll be worth it,' said G-Mamma firmly, but Janey noticed her hands were shaking as she put Trouble down on the floor. Her memories were obviously upsetting her rather a lot.

Alfie was still rather green in the face too. In fact, now she stopped to consider it, her own insides were feeling a little odd. Shaky. Like she might be sick. She sat down on the floor suddenly. 'Do you know something? I think all this whipping backwards and forwards through time and space is bad for us. Dad never got used to it. We're all getting ill.'

'SPIsuit . . .' gasped G-Mamma. 'Suit . . . should . . . prevent . . . nausea . . .'

It was no good. Shoving Trouble out of the way, G-Mamma ran to the toilet. Rosie hastily turned down her SPI-Pod. 'Lordy lord, the past is all coming up,' she said, rather pale herself. 'Can't stand hearing people vomit. Makes me . . .'

And she turned round and threw up in the sink.

Janey walked across and rubbed Rosie's back. It was what her mum did when she was feeling sick, and it always made her feel better. 'If you're ill now, you're going to be much worse when you've gone back through the BELIEVƎ – the Time Slide.'

Rosie nodded, her big blue eyes watery from being sick. 'Be . . . er 'oot,' she mumbled from behind the tissue she was using to wipe her mouth.

'What?'

'I said, I'll make a better suit. Remember me? Rosie B, Everdene's Design Queen?' Rosie twirled around to show them, but staggered off to one side with her hand on her head. 'Yes, indeed. Suit's what I need.'

G-Mamma appeared from the bathroom, leaning heavily on the door frame. 'Well, you've got until tonight, girly-g Rosie B. Then we're packing you off fast, back to the p-p-past.'

Was that a stammer, or a rap? Janey eyed G-Mamma sharply, but her SPI:KE turned around and headed back into the bathroom, almost standing on Trouble. 'Come on, Alfie. Let's leave them to it.'

'Aw,' moaned her friend. 'This is so seriously weird, it's fun. Wait till they start rapping together.'

But Rosie Biggenham stopped him with a chubby paw. 'Not quite sure who you are, sarcastic boy, but the artist has w-w-work to do. Skamoosh.'

Several hours later Janey and her mother entered the Spylab. G-Mamma spun on her bar stool to wave at them and promptly fell off it. She looked dreadful – pale and sweaty, with none of her customary bright make-up on, and her half-closed eyes were bloodshot. 'Oops,' she said indistinctly.

'G-Mamma, have you been . . . drinking?' Janey's mother helped her off the floor.

'I have not! Haven't eaten or drunk anything in hours. Not well,' said G-Mamma, fanning her face.

Trouble pushed a doughnut in her direction, and G-Mamma turned visibly green. 'See? Not even tempted by my old favourite. Re-eallllly sick. Just been sitting here, watching myself sew.'

She pointed to the workbench at which an industrial sewing machine hummed. There was no Rosie B though. At that moment the Wower door opened, and they all turned expectantly. But nobody exited the cubicle, and the door slid closed again.

It wasn't until a familiar voice said, 'Do you think this will w-w-work?' right in Janey's ear that they realized what had happened. Rosie Biggenham was completely invisible, apart from her round blue eyes which were bobbing along beside Janey's shoulder.

'G-Ma . . . I mean, Rosie! We can't see you! Or rather, I can see straight through you.' Janey prodded where she thought the girl's shoulder might be, her finger squashing against some cool-feeling material.

The blue bobbing eyes glanced downwards, and then off to the right as Rosie looked down her arm. 'Lordy lord, I am even more cleverer than what I thought!'

'Told you,' said G-Mamma weakly, too nauseous even to look smug.

'I know! And it was easy,' said the space under Rosie Biggenham's eyes. 'All I did was take some cells from inside the Time Slide with a sieve, and use a shaving from a tortoise's shell because they live

75

just FOREVER, and then zip over to Berty Bert Bert's Spylab in Oz to use a merino-wool spinning machine to make some thread and then weave it into a lightweight gauzy material using Trouble's claws as a rudimentary loom and then cut it out and made a suit and then got in the Wower, and look!' The eyeballs spun as Rosie did a twirl. 'I. Am. A. Genius! Not only will the time cells stand up to the time travel so we don't feel so sick, but I'm invisibubble into the bargain.'

'Invisible,' said Janey, grinning.

'That's what I said. Invisibubble.' The blue eyes fixed on the identical – though bloodshot – ones across the room. 'Hey. Know what I'm thinking?'

'Of course!' said G-Mamma. She tapped out a rhythm with her foot. 'Invisibubble . . .' *Tap tap tap*.

'With the help of Trouble,' rhymed Rosie, clapping her unseen hands as Trouble smugly snapped and unsnapped his peacock tail in time to the beat.

'And never ever ever,' started G-Mamma.

They ended together: 'Have I been more clever!'

G-Mamma sniffed. 'I'm going to miss you, young G, Rosie B, little me.'

The blue eyeballs began to fill up, so Janey grabbed what she thought was Rosie's shoulder. 'Come on. Time to send you home.'

G-Mamma didn't even have the strength to come with them to the garden, so Janey and her mum accompanied the bobbing eyeballs down the stairs and across the grass to the Pet Jet. 'Bye, Rosie,' said Janey. 'I'll programme it and you should pop out in the right era, I think. I'll follow on shortly.'

For one terrible moment it seemed as if one of Rosie's eyeballs had dropped out on to the grass, but then Jean handed Janey the little object she had picked up. 'It's a Spyclops, one of those marbles that Dad created as a boy,' said Janey. 'An early SPI-buy.'

'I think it was delivered by this tortoise that I used for the suit. I found it wandering around near the R-Evolver.' Rosie held it out to them, its head rapidly retracting.

Janey took it. 'Look,' she said, puzzled. There was a name written across its back in black ink. 'Bob. It's called Bob.' Now she looked more closely, she could see more writing beneath the name. It was virtually the same message she'd seen before, but this time in small untidy print. 'EMOC. Come back.'

'It's from Sol – young Dad,' said Janey to her mother. 'He needs me, now. You said I could go back after I'd checked on Copernicus.'

'I know, but it's so dangerous,' Jean sighed. 'Look at what all that travelling has done to your father.'

'There's a solution for that. Rosie,' said Janey, 'you didn't happen to make *two* Invisibubbles, did you?'

invisibubbled

Two pairs of Ultra-gogged eyeballs, one blue and one grey, leaped down the BELIEVƎ helter-skelter towards the era of Geneva Delacroix. To Janey's great relief, the Invisibubbles really worked – the suit seemed to squeeze all her organs in place so that the sick feeling was much reduced. Acupressure points, Rosie B had explained – she'd made them extra tight around the wrists to help with the nausea. Clever, thought Janey.

They popped out, one after the other, into the field behind the Browns' house. As planned, Rosie body-rolled quickly so that Janey wouldn't wallop into her as she landed, but not fast enough. With a squeal, the padded space beneath Janey wriggled, and an indignant, muffled voice yelled: 'Geroff! You're smuffocating me!'

'Sorry!' Janey rolled quickly to one side. It took her a minute or two to locate her new friend; it wasn't until

a pair of crimson Ultra-gogs floated above her face that
she spotted her.

'Up you come, clumsy bum,' said Rosie cheerfully,
and an invisible hand hoisted Janey to her feet.

They looked around. 'Good job we're Invisi-
bubbled,' remarked Janey, pointing towards the back
of the house where a woman was hanging out rows of
blue pyjamas on a long washing line. 'It's broad day-
light.' Casting a longing glance in the direction of her
grandmother, she flicked her eyes towards the gate.

'Come on – if it's daytime, that probably means
Da— Solomon's at school.'

Side by side they Fleet-footed to the gate and out
into the lane. 'This is brilliant!' said Rosie. 'I've always
b-b-been rubbish at cross-country and stuff, but now
it's a breeze. Wheeeeeeeeee!' and she vaulted over a
parked car, leaving a very obvious dent in the bonnet.
Janey laughed. With Rosie getting more G-Mamma-
ish by the minute, it was a doubly good thing that they
couldn't be seen.

Before too long they came to Everdene School; in
moments they had scooted up the front path and into
the clock. Rosie peeled off her Invisibubble balaclava
and her head bobbed around in front of Janey like a
balloon on a string. 'This is amazing!' she said. 'Who
ever knew there was a room back here!'

'Well, Solomon Brown, for one,' said Janey,
shuffling the papers on the desk. 'This is his

79

secret hideout. Look – a Spyclops, and a . . . a copy of the rebus.'

Shoving the piece of paper inside her Invisibubble, Janey pointed up to the stage. 'It's the fashion show,' she said. 'Listen – that's Mrs . . . Maisie Halliday telling you to find the compère again.'

'Yes. I will never forgive that Head Boy of ours for going off sick just at the w-w-worst moment. And he looked fine ten seconds before. Honestly, if he was scared, he just should have said. Anyway' – more of Rosie appeared before her as the girl stripped out of her Invisibubble – 'it's lucky that underneath my wonderful inventionational sensational suit, I'm wearing . . . THIS!'

Janey gasped. The improvised pirate costume from earlier had clearly been through the Wower. Rosie was Glamour Pirate from head to toe, from the shimmering black curls that she loosed from a hairband and shook out like a mermaid's, through to the jewel-encrusted satin shirt in jet shot with silver, and down to the purple silk pantaloons gathered in at her knees into long silver boots.

'Eyelashes!' said Rosie to her Ultra-gogs, and instantly some feathery eyelashes projected themselves on to the glass, framing her eyes as if they were her own. 'Fa-fa-fa-fa – fashion,' she sang in an imitation of her own stammering. 'Hey, that's good. Turn to the left! Right! I should suggest it to someone HUGE, like,

David Bowie!' Rosie slapped on a large beauty spot. 'Excellent. Marilyn Monroe meets Adam and the Ants. Madam and the Pants. Yes!'

'Who?' said Janey. She'd never heard of any of these people. 'Are they spies?

'Never mind, Blondette,' said Rosie with a cheeky grin. 'Just meet the new Rosie B. Wish me luck!'

Moments later . . . 'I'm Rosie B,' called Rosie to the open-mouthed crowds. 'Soon to be the Mamma-G. Now come with me . . .' and she strutted down the catwalk in time to the music, 'and the models . . . You. Will. SEE!' With a drumbeat like a crack of thunder, Rosie pointed a ring-laden black Girl-gauntlet at Geneva Delacroix, who was staring at Rosie agog, and the fashion show began.

Trying not to laugh, Janey jumped out of the way of her young mother, who hadn't noticed the eyeballs floating above centre stage. She eased through the crowd towards Solomon; on Maisie's instructions, he was angling a spotlight away from Geneva and on to the ebullient Rosie B. 'She's the star,' Maisie was hissing.

'What's happened to her?' whispered Solomon. 'It's like she's been transformed in some magical machine . . .' A flash of suspicion crossed his eyes, and for a moment he stared hard at Rosie. Then he shook his head. 'She looks nearly as good as you, Maisie,' he said with a grin.

To Janey's amazement, Maisie Halliday blushed. 'Stop that, Brown, or I'll dock you five house points,' she said.

It sounded like . . . like her dad was flirting with Mrs Halliday. 'Gross!' blurted Janey before she could stop herself. Both Maisie and Solomon jumped, and whipped around in her direction. As quickly as possible, Janey dropped to her knees, taking off her Gogs and shutting her eyes tightly.

'Did . . . ? Did you hear something?' Maisie took a step backwards. Then came a sickening crunch. Squinting, Janey peered down at the floor. 'Oh, look,' Maisie was saying. 'What have we here?'

There lay Janey's trodden-on Ultra-gogs, with one lens splintered and one arm hanging off at a strange angle. With a quick look around, Solomon dropped to his knees and picked them up. 'Those are mine,' he said quickly. 'Must have dropped them.'

But Maisie had already lost interest and had turned back to watch Rosie B leading the model troupe in a strange spiky war dance around the stage, to the huge delight of the baying audience. Solomon put the glasses in his pocket, stared at the people around him one more time, and slipped from the hall.

Janey would have slapped a hand to her forehead if it wasn't for the fact that it would have made a sound. Now he knew that Janey was back in his time – and he was off to look for her. But if his parents waylaid him like last time, he'd end up getting sent to bed – and she'd miss out on the chance to talk to him. Again!

And even though his bike wasn't actually a SPI-cycle, it was souped-up in some way, and unfeasibly fast. If she didn't hurry, he'd get back ahead of her again, which would mean he wouldn't find her, and so he'd have to deliver the message with Bob again. A loop. A time loop. 'This could go on forever,' Janey muttered as she dropped through the trapdoor under the stage, grabbed the shimmering pile of nothingness that was Rosie B's Invisibubble – the future G-Mamma wouldn't be needing it again, after all – and pelted out of the grandfather clock between the great swinging pendulums.

Outside the school doors Janey paused. 'Bike,' she said firmly, before remembering. Only then did she realize just how much she relied on her Ultra-gogs to find things for her. Even without them, however, she was able to spot the one thing that could possibly get her back to the Browns' house before her father.

With a little bounce over the school gates, Janey sprinted after the bus. The doors closed and it pulled away just as she managed to reach it. 'No money anyway,' said Janey, and she hitched a ride the way she had always intended to – invisibly. Eyes squeezed tight against the exhaust fumes and possible detection, she jumped on to the back bumper and clung on to the rear windscreen wiper with her Invisibubble

Girl-gauntlet. As the bus veered around corners and bumped along in fits and starts she held on firmly, trying not to cough. 'There!' She could see him. Solomon was whizzing along the main road on his bike, almost faster than the bus. The bus driver honked at him and Solomon slowed enough to let the bus pass. Janey grinned. That bike was definitely 'special' in some way.

Mistake. As the bus careered past Solomon, she'd instinctively turned towards him as she smiled. The bicycle wobbled dangerously as Solomon gasped at the sight of two grey eyes goggling down at him from the back of the bus. Freaky, thought Janey, wincing as the front wheel of the bike clipped the pavement. The bus groaned its way around the corner and speeded up so there was no chance of her jumping off without killing herself, and Janey lost sight of Solomon. Perhaps he'd fallen off his bike. Perhaps he was injured. Perhaps – perhaps she'd caused that too, and he was genuinely bedridden in his pyjamas. Janey shook her head. Time travel was very, very complicated.

At her stop, Janey dropped down off the bumper and Fleet-footed across to the house, just as the sound of wheels-on-gravel rattled towards her from the end of the lane. Solomon was already striding past the windows, in full view of anyone in the lounge, so she couldn't alert him there. She had to stall for time. *Surprise, surprise, surprise*, thought Janey, remembering

G-Mamma's lesson. Bold as brass, and still invisible, she rapped importantly on the front door.

Her . . . she could hardly even think it . . . grandfather Lancelot Brown threw the door wide open, then, baffled, stepped out on to the porch to look around. Janey dropped behind him and took as long as she dared to look at him. He was tall, very tall, with dark hair faded to a steely grey and intense dark eyes behind big square glasses. He looked clever and kind.

'Who is it, Lance?' her grandmother called out from the kitchen, and Janey had to hold her breath. Right there before her, solid and in the flesh and real life, were the grandparents she had never met. She put her hand over her heart, sure they could hear it beating.

'Don't know, darling,' answered Lancelot slowly, 'but Solomon's just arriving.'

Time to dash. As Carmel Brown trotted down the hall, Janey had to stop herself from grabbing her arm, wanting to whirl her around and tell her what a fabulous son she had, and what an amazing super-SPI, loving husband and wonderful, wonderful dad he would turn out to be . . .

She didn't think Carmel would believe her at the moment. 'Do you think he's finally been expelled?' said the woman with a groan, then she gasped.

'What's the matter?' said Lancelot in his brisk, raspy voice.

Carmel stopped with a hand to her cheek. 'I could have sworn . . . well, that a butterfly just went past me, a grey-blue butterfly, and that . . . somebody kissed my cheek.'

Janey sprinted for the cellar door.

drawn onward

Janey had barely got out of her Invisibubble when there was some outraged yelling in the hallway and Solomon came pounding down the cellar stairs. He put a finger to his lips and closed the door. 'Lunatics! Told them I'm getting some peace down here, away from them. Have you . . . been here all this time?'

'No, I . . . oh!'

She jumped down from her perch as the cardboard box beside her started to move. A mini-earthquake was rattling it along the workbench. Solomon strode over and opened the box. 'It's just Bob.'

Janey breathed a sigh of relief. 'The tortoise!'

'How d'ya know it's a tortoise?'

This time-loop stuff was hard to explain. 'OK . . . this might not make sense, but sometime soon you'll send Bob into the future, with a message on him to me to come back in time to help you.' Solomon stared at her, slowly taking this in. 'Cute name, Bob. Did you call him that because of the palindrome thing? The same backwards and forwards?'

At that Solomon shot her a slightly wicked grin. 'I didn't name him. But you're right, he is the same backwards and forwards. Look.' He lifted Bob out of the box, and the tortoise blinked at her with tiny gleaming eyes. Then Solomon turned him around and thrust his back end under Janey's nose. Someone had drawn a mouth and two eyes on to his tail. He looked like a two-headed tortoise. 'Aren't you, Bob?' said Solomon to the real head. 'Same whichever way you go.'

'I don't think that's very nice,' said Janey, although she had to admit it did look a bit funny.

'Calm down, it didn't hurt him.' Solomon popped Bob back in his box and wiped his own sweating forehead with a large yellow handkerchief. 'I couldn't give him back with any permanent damage, could I? I'm just minding him for Kobi. He's got some big secret project on.'

Janey looked puzzled. 'Kobi? Jakobi Delacroix?' She was hearing that name more and more, and there was something – something peculiar – that she hadn't quite put her finger on.

Solomon sneered. 'How many Kobis do you know?'

'OK, well, even more reason you should be nice to Bob, if he's not yours.'

Rolling his eyes, Solomon said, 'All right, Moan-a-lot. He can have extra lettuce tonight. After,' he said, rummaging in his pocket, 'you help me with this.' He pulled various items from his trouser pockets, then started on his blazer. 'It was . . . What did I do with it? Darn!' he said suddenly. 'I left the rebus in the den. I'd cracked most of it, but there's this funny little letter like a no-entry sign.'

'Don't worry, I've got it.' Janey held out the piece of paper she'd found on the desk under the stage.

Solomon snatched it from her. 'You were there! I knew I saw you, or heard you at school. And on the bus! How—'

'It's too hard to explain,' said Janey. 'Come back again with me to my time, and I can give you a proper look round – at all the gadgets, all the history, all the ways we can travel.'

Solomon's eyes gleamed. 'Everything? Are you serious?'

'Totally,' said Janey. She held up the rebus. 'And we can use the computer to help us work this out.' She didn't know how or when her father had updated the message for his younger self, but she was determined to figure it out.

'You've got a computer? In your house? But only big organizations have computers. You can't have one of your own.'

Janey grinned. 'You really have got to come

with me. Most people in my time have a computer. Some people have two – one on their desk and one to carry around. And thanks to you, I've even got one in my hat, called a PERSPIRE.'

'How will we get past my parents?'

'No problem at all.'

Once Janey had shown him the Invisibubbles, there was no stopping Solomon. He clambered into Rosie B's suit at immense speed, jabbering away at Janey without pausing for breath. 'So they *were* your glasses that Maisie stepped on – what are they called? Ultra-gogs, right, cool. What are the feet things? Right, Fleet-feet. And then you hopped on the back of that bus, and came in here in this . . . Invisibubble, right.' His forehead disappeared as he pulled the balaclava over his head. 'Ha! Did you kiss my mum on the cheek? She was raving like a mad woman when I got home. Why? Why would you do that?'

Fortunately Janey was spared from answering by Solomon's incredulous inspection of his invisible body, which she could interpret from the direction of his intense eyes. 'Cool. Very, very cool,' he said. She could tell from his eyes that he was smiling. 'Not bad, Jane Blonde. Not bad at all.'

Janey smiled back, and the eyes danced across the gloomy cellar. 'Let's go.'

'Follow me.'

Creeping up the stairs that would one day become

the Hallidays' Spylab steps, Solomon eased open the door and rustled through into the hall. As usual, the low voices of his parents could be heard from behind the kitchen door. Janey had the distinct impression from the look in Solomon's eyes that he was making invisible rude gestures in their direction, but she shoved him in the back and together they slipped out of the front door. 'Get a move on,' she whispered. 'Honestly, this is like spying with Alfie!'

Seconds later they were blasting head first up the corkscrew spiral of the BELIEVƎ machine and spurting out into the pre-programmed Jane Blonde time.

All seemed quiet back at her house. 'Who's Alfie?' asked Solomon, as Janey called out into every room via the intercom system that G-Mamma had installed. Suddenly she heard a weak voice in the bedroom below the Spylab. She ran down the SPIral staircase, two steps at a time, pulling off her Invisibubble as she went.

The room was shrouded in darkness, and G-Mamma's terribly bloodshot eyes peered out at her through the gloom. 'There you are,' she groaned hoarsely. 'Bring me broth. I'm sick. Very, very sick!'

Janey ran to the bedside and took G-Mamma's hand. It was clammy and cold, but even more alarming was the way the veins stood out like coils of string glued to the skin. 'How long have you been like this?'

'Long,' sighed G-Mamma. 'Lo-o-o-ong. Help me,' she added plaintively.

'Broth. OK. I'll get Mum to make you some soup,' said Janey.

G-Mamma sat up, alarmed. 'I said help me, not kill me off.'

'Mum's cooking is not that bad,' said Janey. 'I'll go and find her in a minute. I've got Solomon with me.'

But G-Mamma had already sunk back into her pillows, snuggling down into Trouble's warm fur, his amazing tail covering her like an ornate duvet. 'Cream of tomato, please,' she said faintly. Then she began snoring like a road drill.

Janey closed the door gently and whispered into her SPIV. 'Alfie. Halo!'

'I'm here. Where've you been?' Alfie's hair was sticking up at all angles. 'Mum's had me weeding the vegetables as you weren't here.'

'I'm back from the past,' she said. 'I mean forward, I mean . . . you know what I mean. I'm going to show young Solomon around – come over.'

Janey went back upstairs to the Spylab, wondering how Alfie and her dad as a boy would get on. She found Solomon poring over the sheet of paper from the den.

'Is that your computer?' he said, pointing across the room.

Janey laughed. 'No, that's G-Mamma's fridge. This is the computer.' She popped the screen out of the worktop and slid out the panel with the keyboard. 'What do you want to know?'

Solomon stared at the machine, his eyes wide. 'It's so small. How . . . ? Anyway . . .' He thought for a moment. 'Everything! I want to know everything. Who I am . . . all this spying stuff . . . how I become a leader of spies and an ace inventor and scientist . . . I do love science. It's the one thing I'm really good at. But start with this.' He pushed the piece of paper across to Janey. 'Can the computer help?'

She read aloud from the sheet. '"Jane Blonde knows. Believe." You know all that.'

'But what about this?'

Janey peered more closely. It was a tiny sign she hadn't noticed before, perhaps because it was written in a different pen – the same pen that had written on Bob. Paler than the rest of the rebus and less shaky, it consisted of just one letter. She'd seen the letter before, but this time it was in a circle, with a large cross through it. Like a no-entry sign.

Janey studied it for a moment, then brought up the search-engine bar on the Internet page. As Solomon loomed over her shoulder she typed in 'Backward E' and clicked 'Find'.

'There,' she said, clicking on one of the items that appeared on the screen. 'It's a symbol – a mathematical symbol that means "there exists".

Weird. And then there's the sort of no-entry sign. No entry to . . . existence?'

Solomon was looking positively feverish. 'This is . . . incredible,' he said. Janey didn't know whether he meant the computer, or their discoveries, or working with her, but she had to admit it was all pretty exciting. Working with her father. Puzzling out codes that he had written before he had even dreamed them up. Time travel really was quite something. Right then there was a clatter at the door and Alfie barged into the lab, complete with muddy nails and bits of dandelion in his hair. He stopped for a moment at the sight of them both, then stuck out his hand. 'Alfie . . . uh, Agent Halo,' he said, pumping Solomon's hand up and down. 'Honour to meet you . . . sir. Young sir. Sir.'

Solomon looked from Alfie to Janey and back again. 'What does he mean – "sir"?' he asked Janey, extracting his hand from Alfie's. 'I'm barely any older than he is. Is he a bit gormless?'

'Well, your manners improve when you grow up. I'm standing right here,' said Alfie hotly. 'You could talk to me directly, you know. Sir,' he added as an afterthought, though not quite in the respectful tone he'd used before.

'My fault,' said Janey. 'I haven't explained everything. We're about to do a tour. G-Mamma's ill, so would you mind—'

'Staying here and operating the Satispy,' finished

Alfie. He sighed. 'S'pose not. Anything's better than weeding.'

On Janey's instructions, Solomon Wowed up into the spare Invisibubble, and Janey followed. Then, with Alfie pulling a variety of vomit-faces over the grossness of their floating eyeballs, they zoomed off through the skylight to Solfari Lands. There weren't many actual Spylabs left, following the systematic destruction that Janey's father would eventually come to order, but they visited the sites one by one: Seacrest and Argents after Solfari Lands; the Sol's Lols headquarters, the old lab sites in Antarctica and Australia, and even a fly-by on the Tube circuit of the former planet that had been the stronghold and creation of their arch-enemy, Copernicus. The only information she left out was that she was his daughter, and who all the people he went to school with turned out to be. Something warned her that it would be better if those relationships evolved naturally.

'Every single site is one you've created. All the SPI-buys, and the SPIs themselves, are your creations. Apart from this one.'

Solomon stared from the Tube at the lacklustre surface of the planet. 'So this Copernicus character – that enemy monster in the glass case – he made himself a planet? You sort of have to admire him a bit. That is completely cool.'

'Well, not really,' said Janey, pulling him

95

back inside. 'He wanted to use his Lay-Z Beam to take over the world. The universe, even.'

'But we stopped him?'

Janey blushed a little. 'Well, I did. With everything you'd trained me to do.'

'He must have been pretty clever.' Solomon hung on as the SPI-Tube hurtled them towards Florida, the final stop on the Tube system. 'Warped, but clever.'

Janey nodded. 'I suppose so. Not as clever as . . . as you though.' She smiled at Solomon, and he nodded back, thoughtful.

The Tube was slowing as it passed NASA. 'Home soon,' she said. She lowered her head to talk into the SPIV. 'Halo, we're going to get off at Sunny Jim's Swims. Can you Satispy us home from there?'

'No problem, Blonde. Bring some chips from the kiosk. I'm starving.'

'Will do.' Alfie deserved at least that much for patiently transporting them around the universe for the afternoon. 'You know, Alfie's given me an idea. We should see if we can whet G-Mamma's appetite, get some hot doughnuts for her . . . Solomon?'

She looked around, but the tunnel beside her was empty. Either Solomon had fallen out into the heavens, or he'd jumped off the Tube one stop ahead of her.

Panicking, she slid by Tube to the next stop and tumbled out at NASA, to find young Solomon standing before the Squid Man's case. Copernicus looked sick to the core. 'This thing repulses me,' he said softly, leaning his forehead against the glass. 'Yet it's so . . . fascinating. Is this what evil looks like? Do I spend my life fighting this?' He addressed the suspended figure. 'What's wrong with you?' he whispered.

Janey hesitated for a moment, then laid her hand on her boy-father's shoulder. He showed such compassion, even now. 'No need to worry about that,' she said gently. 'He's nearly dead. Barely alive. In fact, I don't think he's got much time left at all. It's for the best.'

The water in the tank was growing cloudy, and Janey hardly dared think about the floating skin cells, the squid ink, the oozing eye fluids that might be causing it to grow murky. He was nearly gone, their enemy. Somehow it made her a tiny bit sad. He'd formed such a big part of her adventures – a terrible, nightmarish part, it was true, but a great enemy in some ways too. Big ideas that in the right hands, or tentacles, could have been wonderful. 'He'll be dead soon,' she repeated.

Solomon's head shot up. 'I need to get home – Squid Man's got the same sickness as my brother. He might be nearly dead too.'

'Your WHAT?' Janey shouted as he sprinted away for the Tube.

'My brother. I'll go on ahead.' His voice was whipped away from her as he disappeared round the corner. 'EMOC, Jane Blonde. Follow me. Help me save him. EMOC!'

'I will,' said Janey, all the time trying to process this new information. Brother? What brother?

less cleverer

By the time Janey got home, G-Mamma had hoisted herself off her bed and was lying on a beanbag. Her skin had a sickly sheen to it, and without her make-up on she looked doubly ill. 'Thought a Wower might help,' she said weakly, flapping a mottled hand at Janey. 'Didn't. Feel worse.'

Janey knelt down beside her. 'G-Mamma, you look dreadful.' Her blonde curls were hanging down in rat's tails on either side of her face, and Janey was alarmed to see how sunken her SPI:KE's cheeks were. 'You're losing weight. You're not eating. Should we get you to a hospital?'

'Are you trying to be funny?' croaked G-Mamma. 'Hospital, because I haven't eaten a doughnut in a few days?'

'Well, maybe you should eat one,' said Janey urgently. 'Doughnuts or ice cream or whatever you fancy.'

G-Mamma pulled a face. 'Can't stand the thought. I can't even . . . rap.'

Janey heard Alfie mumbling something behind her, which sounded like 'You never could rap,' but she spoke over him. 'I'm calling Mum,' she said. 'You're not well. Boy-Dad has gone back already. To his brother, apparently . . . something's not right at all.'

Janey SPIVed Jean Brown, who was over at Alfie's house with Mrs Halliday, discussing tactics for rescuing Boz, and they both agreed to come back instantly. Minutes later they scrambled through the fireplace from Janey's bedroom into the Spylab.

Jean fussed around G-Mamma for a few moments. 'When did it start?'

'Couple of days ago.'

'You were fine when I saw you last, which was . . .' Jean thought for a moment. 'It was when Rosie B was here. She was feeling sick too, come to think of it.'

G-Mamma shrugged wanly. 'But I haven't even done any time-travelling.' Her bottom lip wobbled ominously, and for a second Janey could once more see the nervous Rosie B re-emerge.

Then something occurred to Janey. 'It's meeting Rosie!'

All the heads in the room whipped around to look at her. She ploughed on determinedly, sure she was right. 'Think about it. We all get a bit sick from the travelling, but this is something different. G-Mamma only started developing her symptoms when she met Rosie. They spent hours together.'

Mrs Halliday passed G-Mamma a glass of water. 'Drink this. You look dehydrated. Janey's right, I suspect. It's probably never a good idea to have two versions of yourself in the same room. Or even in the same time.'

'It's my blood,' said G-Mamma, holding out her withered arm with its dreadful rope-like veins. 'Maybe we're sharing it or something. There's something wrong. And now I'm dying! Save me, Janey baby. Save me!'

'You're not dying, Rosie. G-Mamma.' Mrs Halliday corrected herself quickly. But Janey could see in her eyes the same concern that her mother was obviously trying to keep to herself. And a cold hand gripped her heart. G-Mamma was . . . she couldn't bear to think it . . . very sick indeed. And they had no idea what was wrong, never mind the cure. 'Even the Wower didn't help,' she said quietly. She thought of something. 'Maybe it made it worse! Remember how the Wower took what was bad about Copernicus and sort of magnified it? Maybe it took G-Mamma's sickness and did the same.'

It was definitely possible. But there were other urgent things to deal with too. Alfie suddenly looked up from the computer, where he'd been dabbling since his mother came in. 'Oops. Trouble afoot.'

He didn't mean the cat. Pointing at the screen, he told them: 'This is just in from NASA.'

They all stared at the image as he projected it on to the fridge. It was Copernicus's glass case. Empty. 'Someone,' said Alfie, 'seems to have stolen my dad.'

'Or maybe he's died,' said Janey. 'He was looking dreadful. OK,' she added as everyone looked at her, 'even more dreadful.' But just then the last thing her boy-father had said to her popped into her head. 'Oh no,' she said. 'Solomon. He said it was the same – the same sickness that his . . .' She didn't know what he'd meant by it, but now everyone was staring at her so she had to say it. 'He said his *brother* was sick.'

Suddenly there was a roaring sound outside the window. 'The Pet Jet!' shrieked G-Mamma, rolling her eyes like a banshee and attempting to rise from the beanbag in her voluminous white nightie and looking like a ghost from a grave. 'Copper Knickers has risen from the dead and gone back in time.'

Janey rushed to the window, knowing exactly what she would find. 'Solomon!' she hollered across the garden. But her words were swallowed up by the roar of the R-Evolver, spinning, whisking time around in its innards, creating the BELIEVƎ Time Slide . . .

G-Mamma was still flailing around helplessly, trapped by the billowing folds of her Victorian nightgown, and she howled in fury. 'I should go! Let me go after him.'

'You're not going anywhere,' said Jean, and for once G-Mamma didn't argue with her. 'Maisie and I have talked about this – we need to find my husband, especially now that there is a chance that Copernicus has gone back too. We'll go.'

But Janey blocked her mother's route to the Wower. 'No. You can't. You'll get sick, like G-Mamma. Both of you will,' she said, pointing to Mrs Halliday. 'You'll meet yourselves in Solomon's time, and then you'll get the illness too.' She'd stopped them in their tracks. 'I'll go. And don't worry – there's no way Copernicus was fit to do anything.'

'I'll go with Janey,' said Alfie. And she couldn't think of anyone she'd rather have with her on such an important – and strange – mission. 'It makes sense, Mum,' Janey added. 'You can take care of G-Mamma and monitor events everywhere from the Spylab. And you'll be here when we get back.'

Jean considered carefully, then sighed. 'You're right. Absolutely right. OK. Put those Invisibubbles on, won't you?'

So that was it. Mission time.

The whole time he was thrusting his limbs into the Invisibubble Alfie sniggered as he disappeared before his own eyes, until those chocolate-brown eyes were all that were left in view, shaded by his silver Ultra-gogs. Janey whisked through the Wower into hers, wishing that there was some way she could leave her Blonde platinum ponytail sticking out of the back of the headpiece. She even considered ripping a hole in the back of it. Hair waving around on its own might cause a touch of suspicion, however, so there was nothing for it but to allow the Invisibubble balaclava to be tugged down over her head.

'Ready,' she said, watching her mother and Mrs Halliday gulp at the empty air now speaking to them. She picked up the sheet of paper with the rebus on it; across the room, Alfie pulled out two ASPICs and strapped one to each thigh, so they jumped along independently in mid-air. 'Awesome! Double-barrelled!' he crowed, then retraced his steps so he could watch the floating ASPICs in the mirror.

'Work to do, Halo,' said his mother. There was a long pause, in which Janey imagined him sticking out his tongue, waggling his ears and perpetrating any number of rude gestures. Boys! thought Janey. They were all the same! There was a muffled 'C'mon, let's go', and the ASPICs lurched down the SPIral staircase.

Mrs Halliday and her mother came out to see them off. It felt very peculiar not to have G-Mamma there too. 'I don't know how the SPIV will work across time,' said Mrs Halliday, 'but try it anyway. Find some way to let us know you're all right.'

Abruptly she threw her arms out in the general direc-tion of the hovering ASPICs. There was an outraged cry from Alfie. 'That was my chin! What are you doing?'

'Sorry, dear.' Mrs Halliday shuffled uncomfortably. 'Just trying to give you a hug.'

'In public?' Alfie's eyes danced around feverishly. 'Are you completely and utterly stark raving mad?'

But Janey understood. Mrs Halliday was worried about her son. Not surprising really – this was a whole new form of spying that hadn't yet been thoroughly tested. 'I can't see you, you know, Alfie,' Janey told him, giving her own mother a kiss goodbye.

'So? I'm still not hugging her.' Alfie sounded distinctly put out, but after a moment Janey heard a gentle smacking sound, and from the corner of her eye she saw Mrs Halliday put a hand to her cheek, just like her grandmother had done. It was a good job she was invisible, or Alfie would have seen the grin that spread across her face as she pushed the button to GINA BELLARINA time.

'It's like one of those water slides at Sunny Jim's,' she warned Alfie, 'only without the water. You'll get pretty dizzy. I'll go first so I can grab you if you miss the exit.'

'I won't though.'

'Just in case.'

'Yeah, but I won't . . .'

'Get on with it,' cried Mrs Halliday and Jean together, and Janey, laughing, jumped into the R-Evolver's cylinder of dark-light.

She slithered head first down the BELIEVƎ

slide, twisting and spinning so fast that occasionally she corkscrewed right around inside the tube. The GINA turn-off was approaching; she felt a tug on the upper half of her body, and suddenly she was veering off to the left, flipping over and over inside the tunnel, then spilling out on the ground next to the tractor tyre.

Behind her there was a roaring sound. No, not a roaring sound. An actual roar. Alfie was screaming. Rolling out of the way, Janey got to her feet ready to catch hold of him as he shot out of the BELIEVƎ machine making the most enormous racket. 'Shut up!' hissed Janey, following the noise and clamping a hand over the space below his Ultra-gogs. 'Secret mission, remember?'

Alfie shook her hand off, blathering ecstatically. 'But that was fantastic! Amazing! Let's do it again! Where else does it go? Ow!' The grip from Janey's Girl-gauntlet clamped his jaw shut. Once Janey was sure he'd calmed down, she let go. 'All right. I'll be quiet. Where do we go now?'

Janey looked around. 'It's night-time. The house, I suppose.'

Alfie set off towards it and stopped abruptly. 'Hang on. That's *my* house.'

'I know. In the past the Brown family lives here. It sounds like they have for many generations.' Janey pushed him on. 'There's not even a school here yet.'

The house was in darkness as they approached.

Janey guided Alfie around to the back and whispered to him: 'Cellar. I think that's the best way to get in. But it's always locked.'

'Wait a minute.' As she watched, the APSICs swayed off across the yard to the washing line. A surge of dust flew up from next to the post holding up the line, and then, to Janey's surprise, a large key floated across the garden towards her. 'Emergency key. Apparently Mum wasn't the first to use that hiding place,' said Alfie in her ear, and then the key fed itself into the lock and turned, and the door fell open.

Janey followed the sound of Alfie's footsteps into the cellar and closed the door behind her, pulling off her balaclava as Alfie did the same. The two heads looked around the room. 'Creepy,' said Alfie. 'So do you reckon young Sol brought Squid Man back to experiment on him?'

'No! Why?'

'Because this is exactly where I'd stash a dead body if I had one.'

'He might not be dead though.'

'Don't spoil it for me,' said Alfie, but Janey was sure she could sense a little tinge of concern in his voice.

They peeked around the shelves and plant pots, but of Copernicus there was no sign. The only living thing in the room was Bob, scuffling around among the lettuce leaves in the bottom of his cardboard box. Janey lifted him out and showed Alfie his drawn-on tail, and Alfie snorted. 'Ha! That's hilarious. Come on, you've got to admit, that's a bit funny.'

'It's mean,' said Janey. 'Oh, look! The symbol's changed again.' Just under the nose, the word EMOC had been crossed through.

'What is your dad playing at?' Alfie tilted his head thoughtfully. 'Mind you, he's always done his experiments like that – first on himself, or on some friendly animal: Trouble, the frog-mouse thing, Monkey Boy Twelve . . .'

'Stop it!' said Janey. 'That's not true! Or . . .' Actually it was true. But he'd meant no harm. 'He was only ever trying to make things better. It was your dad who did all the horrible stuff, like cloning sheep, and turning monkeys into people in the first place. Don't go blaming my dad.'

Alfie shoved his disembodied face into hers. 'Well, don't blame mine either.'

'Why not?'

'Because he must have had his reasons, OK?'

'No,' shouted Janey. 'It's not OK! Your . . . father is very, very bad, and mine's only ever done things for good. You know that!'

But just as Alfie was about to retort, the kitchen door flew open, and a smooth voice interrupted them. 'Children, children . . . good job it was me and not my parents.' Solomon trod down the stairs in his blue pyjamas and slippers, a faint grin on his face as he turned the key in the door and pocketed it. 'Best keep them out. They might get a bit of a shock, seeing two heads bouncing around their cellar.'

Janey was flooded with relief. 'Solomon, thank goodness it's just you. Sorry, we were just having a bit of an arg . . .'

'I heard. That old argument: my dad's bigger than your dad.' Solomon smiled again.

'It wasn't like that.'

Judging by the twitching of the ASPICs, Alfie was shuffling uncomfortably. 'Actually, I suppose it was a bit like that. I was just going to say you're right, Blonde. About your dad.'

'Oh. Thanks. OK,' said Janey in a small voice.

Solomon was gazing at Alfie's floating head with a look of puzzlement. Then he shook himself. '*So how's your brother, Solomon? What's the matter with him, Solomon?* Feel free to ask any time you like.'

'Sorry,' said Janey quickly. 'How is your brother? In fact . . . who is your brother?'

'His name is Bowood. I thought you knew all about my family, Jane-Blonde-Who-Knows.' Solomon sat down on the cellar steps, suddenly looking a bit pasty. 'You know – the old family history. How Lancelot Capability Brown submerged the village of Mannings Hill to create a massive lake, turned it into a little lost city of Atlantis.'

109

Janey stared. 'I didn't know that, no. He drowned a village?'

'There was nobody in it!' Solomon laughed. 'We're not that bad.'

Alfie's head bobbed towards Janey. 'I thought your family were all spies.'

'I don't know about *her* family,' said Solomon, shrugging again. Janey held back a groan – Alfie had almost given the game away. 'But my relatives are gardeners. That's why we have these weird names: Dad's called Lancelot, like the original Capability Brown. That's my name too as the older son, though I use Solomon to avoid confusion. And Bowood's named after the village that sprang up after great-granddaddy-grandad-wotsit drowned Mannings Hill.'

'Fascinating,' said Alfie. 'But why did you suddenly run off from NASA?'

Solomon stared at him insolently. 'Keep up, Alfie. I already told you. Bowood's sick. I came back to check on him. It's the same disease as Copernicus has, by the looks of it. Seemed to me we could discover a cure by studying the Squid Man, seeing as he's nearly dead anyway. Or Bowood could. He's cleverer than me, and I thought if he could see Monster Mash, even as sick as he is, Bowood might be able to work out a cure for himself.' Solomon sighed as if the conversation was becoming very boring. 'He's capable of it. The brilliant Bowood Brown.'

Brilliant Bowood Brown. That reminded her of something. Brilliant Bowood Brown . . .

As they stared, Solomon walked back up the stairs and slammed the door shut behind him.

Somehow Janey knew it was going to be locked tight.

III

12 bowood bother

'What's going on?' Alfie's head swivelled towards the door and then back to Janey. 'Since when has your dad had an actual real-life brother? And where's he gone? Why's he locked us in? What is *up* with that dude? He's got an attitude. Oh no, I rhymed. But anyway. What's his problem? I thought he needed your help.'

'I don't know,' said Janey. Every question Alfie was voicing was rattling around in her brain too. One thing was for certain – being able to see only someone's head was very distracting, making it even more difficult for her to think properly. 'We've got to get out of these Invisibubbles.'

Alfie waggled his balloon-like head. 'No way. I'm thinking we should put our balaclavas back on. We've got to get out of here somehow, and these are our best disguise.'

'We'll keep them with us, OK? But if I need your help I'd rather be able to see you.'

'Fair enough.'

Either side of the flower pots, they took off their Invisibubbles. Feeling much more normal in her everyday silver SPIsuit, Janey rattled the door handle. 'Completely locked.' Next she foraged under the tarpaulin behind the flower pots. 'This should be the tunnel entrance. Takes us right through to Everdene. Just . . .'

She lifted up the tarpaulin completely and gawped. 'It's gone! Someone's filled it in.' The tunnel through which she had reached the school on her last visit had disappeared, the surface rough with new concrete. On closer inspection, there was a special reason it was rough. 'Alfie, look.'

Drawn in thick strokes about the width of her finger was the now familiar sign:

'I think it means . . . the answer isn't this way,' said Janey.

'Well, it definitely means no exit. SPInamite it,' said Alfie, reaching into his pocket for his detonating gum.

'I . . . I don't think we need to!'

Janey jumped backwards as the concrete shook beneath her feet. 'Earthquake?' she called to Alfie, who was trying to stop the tower of flower pots from toppling over. A crack appeared across the symbol; with a quick glance at each other, Alfie stood poised with his Boy-battler ready to biff whoever it was into kingdom come, and Janey flicked out her titanium blade, steadying Bob's box as it shuddered on the nearby workbench. 'Come on then, you big mole,' said Alfie through gritted teeth as the concrete splintered before their very eyes . . .

The creature that emerged did look like a big mole, with brown fur, blinking eyes and a waffling nose. Only when it let out an enormous sneeze, trumpeting 'WERRRRCH!' so loudly that it blew some of the dust off, did they recognize who had popped out of the floor.

'Rosie!'

Janey pulled the future G-Mamma to her feet. Her body was encased in what looked like the school caretaker's overalls, spray-painted with symbols and images from the future. EVƎ, Bob, JB, G-MAMMA: all were scribbled across her limbs in lurid colours. Across her shoulders was an incredible depiction of a gold-and-tawny cat with go-faster stripes and the words 'ROSIE B LOVES TROUBLE' emblazoned beneath it in sequins. Her hair was no longer in plaits but cascaded instead in glossy brown curls down the back of her head, clipped tightly into the sides above her ears with two sparkly hairslides.

'You've got a curly mullet,' said Alfie, trying not to

laugh, but thankfully Rosie either didn't hear or didn't understand.

'So this is where it goes!' Rosie shook herself like a wet poodle, not seeming at all surprised to see Janey and Alfie there. 'I was just, er, at school, ch-checking out that den place you disappeared into, and lookee here: a tunnel into the future!'

'Ah.' Now Janey understood why she was so matter-of-fact about them being there. 'No, actually you're still in your own time. We've travelled back to you, not the other way round. And now Solomon Brown seems to have locked us in the cellar.'

'Well, he would, w-w-wouldn't he? Full of himself, as always.' Rosie looked less than impressed at the mention of his name.

That didn't make sense. In the future G-Mamma adored Janey's father. 'Right,' said Janey, taking a deep breath. 'I think it's time we told you everything, and you can help us sort it out. Because, just at this moment, we're very confused.'

Ten minutes later, after scribbling family trees in the dust, Rosie sat back on her heels. 'Right. I'm G-Mamma. Solomon Brown is your dad, and Geneva is your mum, Jean, who I met, and you –' she pointed at Alfie – 'your mum is Maisie Halliday, and your dad is a squid called something Knickers.'

'He wasn't always a squid,' said Alfie, rolling his eyes. 'And I don't suppose he was always called Knickers either. Whatever. Anyway, who are *your* parents?'

Rosie shrugged. 'Dinner lady and the caretaker. Or they were till they were killed in a car accident with Geneva's parents. That's how I got into Everdene. C-c-couldn't afford it otherwise.' For a split second her stammer returned as she recalled her humble beginnings, but she sniffed a couple of times and poked at the name of Janey's dad. 'So Sol really becomes your dad?'

'Yes. And the older version of him is stuck here somewhere in the past – if only I could just get out of this stupid cellar and look for him!'

Suddenly Alfie put a finger to his lips and jerked his thumb towards the ceiling. Over their heads someone was pacing. The steps stopped, and Janey could almost picture the person above cocking their head towards the floor, wondering about the noise beneath their feet. In the next moment there came an outraged roar. 'SOL-O-MON!'

Two more pairs of feet. One light, tapping. Another more shuffling. Carmel first, then Solomon.

Janey leaned in. 'Rosie,' she whispered, 'are you ready to start being a fully fledged spy?'

With a glint in her eye, Rosie planted her hands on her hips like a superhero ready to launch. 'Whatever you may say, Rosie B will save the day.'

'Good, because I've got a plan. Quick!'

In about ten seconds Alfie and Janey had each put on their Invisibubbles. They crept up the cellar stairs towards the din of the argument going on in the kitchen. Then, with a wink at Rosie as the signal, they crouched down, ready for action, and lowered their faces so that their Gogs wouldn't be spotted in the darkness.

Right on cue, Rosie started to holler: 'Let me out! I don't deserve this! Solomon, you're a very, very mean boy, and I'm going to tell the headmaster about you locking me in like this! I won't do it! I won't do your homework for you!'

As Janey had predicted, the cellar door flew open and three faces appeared. 'What the devil . . .' started Lancelot Brown, as Carmel staggered back, aghast, and Solomon's intense eyes grew wide at the sight of Rosie Biggenham trapped in his cellar. By him, apparently.

'What are you doing here?' he said, not even having to act mystified.

'Nothing!' Rosie shook her fist dramatically. 'Certainly not your homework. Mr Brown, Mrs Brown, I just won't do it. Just because I get a s-s-scholarship to Everdene and I've got d-d-dead parents and I st-st-stutter sometimes, he thinks he can force me to do his homework for him. It's like s-s-s-slavery!'

Solomon turned to his parents, hands up, to declare himself innocent. Meanwhile, Janey and Alfie crept one by one through the trio and out into the kitchen. As she crouched along, Janey felt her grandmother's hand come into contact with the back of her head, and she dropped down still further, belly-crawling on the lino past the large kitchen table as Rosie distracted the Browns with more wailing and moaning, and Solomon tried to explain the unexplainable to his father, who was pounding the door frame, shouting, 'You've done it this time, Lancelot Solomon Brown! This time it's too much! Oh, you've really done it now!'

'Darling, you can't go incarcerating young women in the cellar.' Carmel Brown sounded close to tears. 'You'll get . . . arrested. Her parents must be terrified. Oh, darling, you silly, silly boy.'

'But I didn't . . .'

Janey was just starting to feel sorry for him when she remembered that while he was innocent of this particular charge, he hadn't shied away from incarcerating her. Straightening up in the hallway, she found Alfie's dark eyes waiting for her at the bottom of the stairs. She followed.

Alfie turned instinctively towards his own bedroom at the end of the long landing. But when he opened the door he staggered and held on to the door frame. Janey ran as he exhaled shakily, tearing off his balaclava. 'It's . . . He's . . .'

The thing on the bed seemed barely alive. The long, sinuous limbs were mottled like mouldy cheese, shot through with the same terrible twisted veins that criss-crossed G-Mamma's arms. Even the yellow eye the size of a dustbin lid was turning red with blood, while the other, human, one was closed tight, a gummy seal sticking the eyelids together. The rise and fall of the Squid Man's chest and the sound of his raspy breathing had all but stopped, but a slow, shuddering pulse was still visible in the knobbled veins. How long would he survive out of his tank?

Janey had taken off her balaclava too. Alfie turned to her, his face bleak. 'As soon as I get home,' he said hoarsely, 'I'm changing bedrooms.' But there was no venom in his words. None of the usual hatred for his father.

There was a sound – a moan – nearby and they made their way to the next bedroom. As she couldn't see Alfie's arm, Janey tugged on the thick lock of hair hanging out of the nape of his neck. 'Whose room is this in your house?' she whispered. Alfie shook his head. Nobody's. 'Just junk,' he whispered back.

They opened the door slowly. The junk room had once been a boy's bedroom. And a boy in blue pyjamas was huddled in the corner of the room, wedged up against the headboard, his thin veiny arms wrapped around his knees. Was *this* her father's brother?

He turned in fear as they crept into the room, and Janey could have kicked herself for forgetting what they must look like. Two heads, one dark, one blonde, floating along on their own. With any luck, the boy would believe it was part of the fever he so clearly had, his dark hair slick with sweat, his eyes rimmed with scarlet.

But as soon he'd seen them the panic in his eyes subsided and he dampened his lips, ready to speak. 'You came,' he whispered, his voice little more than a breath. 'Thank you!'

As if speaking to his pillow, he dropped his head on to his chest. 'She's here!'

And then he smiled up at Janey, and she found herself looking into a pair of bright blue eyes. Eyes she'd seen before – that she knew very well indeed.

But just as her brain was struggling to take this in, a hand shoved her in the back. She flew headlong into the room. Beside her, Alfie's head dropped to the floor – he too had been pushed into the room. The door clicked shut behind them, and she scrambled backwards towards the bed.

Solomon turned the key in the lock and held it up for Janey and Alfie to see, then strode over to the bed. 'I got them, like I said I would. It'll be OK now, little brother. You'll get better now.'

The boy on the bed nodded gratefully as Solomon turned down the top of the quilt. 'Come on now. Back into bed. You need to keep warm. In you go, Bowood.'

The younger boy – not that much younger, but weakened and shrunken from his terrible illness – collapsed on to the bed as Solomon Brown stood up triumphantly. 'I promised him, see. Promised him I'd get you. I followed all his instructions, even how to programme the BELIEV∃, and I found you.'

'But –' Janey stopped herself. She had thought that the instructions had been her father's. That he, in his caveman state, was waiting for her to come and rescue him. Had she really got it so wrong?

Alfie ripped off the top half of his Invisibubble, and his torso moved over to sit on the chair at the desk. 'All right. Well, we're here now. What can we do?'

'Stay,' said Solomon. 'You just have to stay.' He smiled. 'I've worked it out. Even me – the not-so-clever one. He gets better *because* you stay. It means you'll get sicker, like Squid Man next door, but he'll get better. You will. I promise you, Bozzy.'

He smiled fondly at his brother as Janey watched him, her stomach twisting far more than it ever had on the BELIEV∃ machine. The boy Solomon was nuts. It was quite clear.

And then it hit her.

Sol wasn't the one who would become her father.

She looked at the boy in the bed.

Bowood. Bowood Bozzy Brown. Brilliant Bowood Brown. Boz Brilliance Brown.

This was her father.

And he was dying.

so and bo

Janey stared. The eyes should have told her something earlier. She had only ever really noticed that Sol's eyes were intense, not that they were a dark rich brown. Not blue as a summer sky, like Boz's.

'I don't understand,' she said plainly, when the staring had gone on for an uncomfortable length of time. 'Bowood is Boz, your younger brother, but it was *you* who was in the den and came to the future to find me.'

Solomon clapped Boz lightly on the back. 'All his doing. He sent me. And Bob. I didn't even know about the den, let alone that time machine. But when he started to get sick, he needed my help. Didn't you, little brother?' He smiled fondly at Boz, sadness misting his eyes.

So it *was* her father (her young father) who had written out the rebus and explained the programming of the machine to his big brother, even when he could barely speak. Boz Brilliance Brown had started young. Janey didn't know which way to turn, so shocked was she by all these revelations. She'd come to find her grown-up dad, but had ended up discovering so many secrets instead . . .

Boz squirmed on the bed, a strange combination of shyness and illness. Talking was obviously too much of a strain, so he held out his hand to Solomon, who passed him a pen. He wrote on his own shaking hand and held it out for them to read.

'"JB 2 EMOC." That's right. That's what you told me, isn't it? Find this JB person,' said Solomon.

Janey turned to Boz. 'Is that right? Will you get better now?'

The boy Boz looked up at her through his dark, matted eyelashes and gave a tiny shake of the head. Then he wrote again on the palm of his hand. B4. He added another word. EVE. Before eve. Did that mean before evening?

Solomon jumped off the bed. 'Boz, I'm just going to lock you in next door with the Monster Mash, and you'll start getting better soon. I did, as soon as the squid thing got more sick. Look.' He held out his own hand. It still had a sinewy look about it, but was nowhere near as horrific as Bowood's crazed claws.

'Er . . . why exactly do you think the squid will improve your brother's health?' asked Alfie. 'You complete madman,' he added under his breath.

Solomon turned his head sharply, eyeing Alfie then Janey carefully as if weighing something up. 'I don't think . . .' he said slowly, with just a hint of menace, 'that you really want to question me. Not seeing as I become your boss and everything.'

'You so do not,' said Alfie rudely. He pointed to Boz. 'He does.'

Boz rallied for a moment to gaze at Alfie. He looked terrified. It hardly seemed possible that this sickly boy would become the great SPI and leader they knew and loved. But it had to be the case – the puzzles, the genius mind, the blue, blue eyes . . .

Solomon faltered, then turned to Janey. 'Tell him. Tell your little friend here everything you told me about who I become, and all the things I invent, and all the . . . important, clever stuff that I do. It's about time, as well. Always second best. Even though I'm older.' He cuffed Boz gently around the head. 'Not that I mind, because he's my baby brother, and he's amazing, but . . . tell him anyway!' Solomon pushed between Janey and Alfie, breathing angrily into her face.

'But . . .' Janey didn't know how to start. She *had* told him all those things. She'd led him round the Spylabs, introducing him to all of Boz's brilliant creations. But she'd got it horribly wrong. 'I'm sorry, Solomon. I didn't know you really existed. I thought you were Boz using Solomon as an alibi. Alfie's right.

It's . . . It's not you that goes on to do all those things. It's him. Your brother. The real Boz.'

She couldn't have had more effect on Solomon if she'd stabbed him with her titanium blade. Reeling, he dropped the key and staggered back towards the wardrobe. 'No,' he said hoarsely. His voice gathered strength. 'Impossible! How can that be true? He's little, and he's . . . he's sick! Boz can't become all of those things. He can't! It should be me!'

'He's lost it,' hissed Alfie, grabbing the dropped key. 'I'll go for help.' He headed down the landing as the noise in the bedroom reached a crescendo.

But the full horror of the situation was sinking in even as Solomon thrashed around the room. Janey watched him, cogs turning in her mind. The thing in the next room was dying. And the worse it got, the more energy Solomon seemed to have.

'You're . . . him,' she whispered, her eyes flicking unconsciously towards the other room. 'That's why you're becoming well again as he dies. Two versions in the same time. Copernicus. You're him.'

Solomon stopped short, even his breathing hanging in the air. Then, slowly, he turned his hand over, his dark eyes clouding with pain and tears as he saw that the twisted veins were smoother still. He was getting better. 'No . . .' he groaned, falling to his knees. 'That . . . despicable . . . that *thing* . . .' And suddenly he lunged at the bed. 'NO!'

In his fury as he got up he yanked at the wardrobe door; to the horror of everyone in the room it toppled forward, straight into his face, the sharp corner slicing into his flesh. Blood spurted through his fingers as a dreadful gash split his top lip almost in two. Janey grabbed him by the arm and pulled him clear as her Girl-gauntlet held up the top of the wardrobe. She heaved and strained to get it upright again as Solomon howled in pain and rage and tore at Boz's sheets, trying to stem the flow of blood from his face. As the dark stain seeped through the cotton, it suddenly became clear where the scar that disfigured his face later in life had come from. It had come . . . from her, Janey thought with a sob. Today.

Solomon was raving now, incapable of taking in what he had just learned but unable to dispute the evidence. As his tears mingled with the blood on his face, he lifted a finger to his poor brother, whose pain was every bit as sharp. 'You! You get all the glory. You become this spy, this super-SPI. You've always had everything so easy. Why do you get this too? Why?' And he leaped to his feet, suddenly looking every bit as menacing as the man-squid he would become. 'And I turn into a sea monster. The Monster Mash. Why! It's not fair, Bowood. It's not fair!'

Footsteps. Coming up the stairs. 'Alfie,' whispered Janey hopefully, and she slid down beside the wardrobe, pulling on her balaclava. Alfie had met trouble; backing into the room, he hauled open the wardrobe door and jumped inside, struggling with his own Invisibubble balaclava, but there was no time to drag the top half of his Invisibubble up over his body.

'Solomon Brown, I swear that if you . . .'

Lancelot and Carmel launched themselves into the room. Even though they couldn't possibly see her, mostly invisible and behind the wardrobe, Janey held her breath as they looked around at the devastation. Her heart almost stopped as Carmel Brown peered into her son's open wardrobe. Alfie would be spotted! But then through the crack in the door, she saw what he had done: opening his arms, he'd stood sideways, stock still. With no head, hands and lower body visible, he looked for all the world like a jumper on a hanger. Carmel shut the door abruptly as Lancelot hauled Solomon to his feet and out on to the landing.

'Have you hurt him?' he demanded bitterly.

Solomon pushed his hand away. 'No – this is my blood!' he protested. 'Mine! Bowood's sick, but I'm helping him. . .'

When Carmel followed them out to the upstairs hallway, Janey followed too on her hands and knees. Her grandmother's pace slowed as she pushed open Solomon's bedroom door. Beside her, Janey felt Solomon slump. This would be the last straw.

'Solomon – what in the name of all creation

127

is that?' she whispered, taking in the warped, twisted figure of Copernicus on the bed.

'It's . . . a . . . I don't know,' stammered Solomon. 'I brought . . . I brought him for Bozzy, to help cure Bozzy's disease . . .'

But Carmel started to cry, and Lancelot thrust Solomon away from him as he reached out for his wife. 'That's enough, my boy,' he said quietly, in such a terrible tone that Janey felt her stomach twist for Solomon. 'The sickness. What the doctor said about your ravings. First, locking that girl in the cellar – poor, poor thing – and now this . . . creature. You need looking after – professionally.'

'You don't get it!' A sob caught in Solomon's throat. 'I've just been trying to help. Bozzy's the one – the one with the wild ideas and the wicked inventions. You have no idea what he'll become. You have to believe me. You have to!' he screamed, as Boz moaned from the bedroom behind.

Minutes later there was the flash of blue lights through the front door, followed by a sharp rap. 'Who's that?' Solomon tried to evade his father's grip, but he had too tight a hold on his sleeve.

'These people will help you, Solomon,' said Carmel, her voice catching in her throat. 'Please don't shriek so . . . when you're better you can come home.'

'I'm not sick! I'm not!' Solomon grappled for his mother's hand as Lancelot called out for the people at the door to come in, to take Solomon. 'Don't, Mother. Don't send me away!' His head whipped around, desperately. 'Bowood!' he screamed, desperate. 'Tell them! Help me! Jane Blonde, you can stop it . . . do something!'

Trying not to cry, Janey scuttled backwards into Boz's bedroom, wrenching off her balaclava. Boz was rocking in anguish on the bed, his head down, his tragically thin arms wrapped around his knees. Janey shoved his feet. 'Help him! He's being carted off to the mad house or something. Help him, Boz!'

Boz lifted his head, tears coursing down his face, as Alfie stumbled out of the wardrobe. 'Ca-can't . . .' He pointed to his throat.

'He can't speak,' said Alfie, handing him a pen. 'Write it then. What can we do?'

'Go on, Dad,' said Janey. 'You know who I am, don't you?'

Crying silently, Boz nodded and wrote on the palm of his hand. He held it out, shaking, to Janey.

G E N E V A

'Come on,' said Janey to Alfie, trying to cut out the sound of Solomon being dragged down the stairs, out to the waiting ambulance, accompanied by the tortured sobs of her grandmother. 'GENEVA – we've got to find my mum.'

geneva

'This way!' shouted Alfie's Ultra-gogs, spinning off to the left outside the front door.

Janey ran after him, closing her ears to Solomon's outraged cries from the back of the ambulance: 'There! The glasses! Floating spectacles near the garage – it's two spies from the future, Jane Blonde and Alfie Agent Halo. I'll kill you, you stupid secret agents! You and your mastermind up there. You'll be sorry you crossed me! He won't win this time. Get your hands off me – I am NOT raving!'

He sounded like a complete madman. Janey didn't like to think about what might happen to him when he got to wherever they were sending the ambulance. Poor Solomon. He'd been fine all along really. Misunderstood – a bit quirky and prickly maybe – but fine. As she saw where Alfie was headed, she had an idea. If she showed Sol they were still trying to help him, gave him a sign of their faith, perhaps she could prevent him from turning into the monster he would be in the future. 'You start the car,' she said as the glasses hovered near the door of a sleek, low-slung sports car, 'but give me your Boy-battler first.'

Alfie was too busy emptying out the glove compartment to answer, trying to find the keys, but Janey felt along the dashboard for his other hand and ripped off his spy-glove. 'Lock and Load your Gogs on mine,' she said, 'and collect me when you come past the ambulance.'

'If I ever find the . . . ah.'

Janey lowered her eyes and sped off across the front garden, weaving between her shaking grandparents, seeing off their son, and the medical team who were struggling to hold him down. She only lifted her head as she got to the back of the ambulance.

'Solomon,' she said firmly. He whipped around, searching for the voice, and fixed on her glasses. 'We don't need to be enemies. Take this.' She thrust the Invisibubble Boy-battler into his hand just as an engine growled into life behind them. As Solomon began to splutter, 'Th-there, look – I told you!' Janey swivelled her head towards Alfie so he could see her glasses, and the car raced towards them. The door flew open beside her and she threw herself into the passenger seat; then they tore from the yard, leaving a small crowd of people watching a car drive off completely on its own.

'Uh, Alfie – when did you learn to drive?' Janey asked suddenly. It certainly hadn't been in any of the training they'd had so far.

'It was the one and only test that Mum could never pass,' he said, wheel-spinning around a corner towards the town. 'She's a danger to everyone behind a wheel. So she had me learn when I was eight or nine. Very useful it's been too. Right, obviously we're going to fetch your mum, who I gather is this Geneva person. Where is she?'

Janey gasped. 'Oh! I don't know. Where do you think she lived?'

'Search me.' Alfie slowed the car as they pulled up to a crossroads. 'That way to town. Other way to Everdene.'

She had no idea. 'Gogs,' said Janey, 'home for Geneva Delacroix.'

It was asking a lot of them, to work out who this person was, back in time, and find her address across the decades. 'Oh,' said Janey. 'It's showing me my house. No,' she said loudly, 'Geneva Delacroix.'

'Are you sure they're not the same place?' said the space in the driver's seat. Janey could hear Alfie tapping on the steering wheel.

The same place – well, anything was possible. 'Give it a go,' she said.

They raced through the quiet streets. There was a lot less traffic in her parents' time, and in just a few minutes they were pulling up outside her home. It looked smarter than in her day, with new paint and a neatly clipped hedge. Janey sighed. How she wished G-Mamma would appear across that hedge, rapping and eating and generally being mad. She wasn't even able to SPIV her – or was she? Janey pulled off her Invisibubble and reached for her SPI Visualator. 'G-Mamma, are you there?'

Her SPIV buzzed back at her.

'G-Mamma, I said are you—'

'YES!' came the buzz, more distinctly this time.

Janey turned the SPIV upside down so she could see her SPI:KE's face. It was gaunt, pale, with dreadful spiderwebs of scarlet criss-crossing the cheeks and the whites of the eyes. 'You look awful, G-Mamma,' whispered Janey.

'Sick as a sausage,' agreed G-Mamma hoarsely. 'EMOC, Zany Janey.'

Janey smiled. 'I will. Just have to sort things out. I'll come back soon.'

To her horror, a vast tear splurged down G-Mamma's sunken cheek. 'OK. Do your stuff . . .' She broke into a coughing fit as she pulled something into view. 'He's waving, doing a little fan dance for you with his uber-tail,' whispered G-Mamma.

A sabre claw was glinting in the background, and behind it what looked like a field of corn swayed left and right as the Spycat waved his tail at her.

That was the buzzing sound – Trouble purring. It was heartbreaking.

Alfie's elbow hit Janey near the temple as he pulled his Invisibubble off over his head. 'Let's get a wiggle on, Blonde. I don't think anyone's going to last very long at this rate.'

'I'll EMOC soon,' Janey promised her SPI:KE. 'Very soon.'

If they had the right house, of course. Dressed in their visible, everyday SPIsuits, Janey and Alfie marched up the garden path, and Janey rapped on the familiar front door with her Girl-gauntlet. Even before she'd finished knocking the door swung open, and a strapping sandy-haired teenage boy stared out at them, tossing his ridiculously long fringe out of his eyes. 'Come in,' he said.

Janey and Alfie looked at each other. 'You don't even know who we are,' said Alfie.

'Yeah, I do,' said the boy. 'I've been following you. Well, parts of you.' He pointed to Janey's Ultra-gogs.

'You're the Head Boy . . .' said Janey, remembering.

He stuck out a hand and grasped Janey's own in a very firm handshake. 'Jakobi Delacroix – Kobi. I've been watching you since you turned up before the fashion show. Some strange stuff going on, eh? You been getting my messages?' His vividly pale blue eyes sparkled mischievously.

The Spylets gazed at the older boy. So this was Jakobi, Head Boy, Geneva's brother, and owner of Bob, and best friend of Solomon Brown. Janey stared at him again. Geneva's brother? Wouldn't that make him . . . Uncle James? What messages? And why would he have been sending them to her?

'Whenever you're ready,' he said cheerfully.

'Sorry! Yes. We need to see Geneva.'

'Right. I'll come with you.' Jakobi shook Alfie's hand as they stepped inside, and he led the bewildered pair up the stairs to Janey's own bedroom.

Geneva was perched on the end of the bed, chatting animatedly to Maisie Halliday, who was coiled up on a rug on the floor, still holding her clipboard. 'I always knew it was you that he . . . Kobi! Get out.'

'Aw. Love you too, sis,' said Kobi with that same smooth, easy cheerfulness.

'You're so weird, Kobi. Did you ever wonder if you were adopted?'

He grinned. 'No. But I thought you were.'

Geneva turned to Maisie. 'Do you know, he's so vain about that fringe that he won't even go out on a windy day.'

'Don't be rude. I've brought some people to see you.'

Geneva jumped up, surprised. 'Oh! Jane Blondette. Nice to see you – how did you know where I . . . ? Maisie, what's up?'

Maisie Halliday had stood up and was now standing face to face with Alfie, who was doing his best not to gawp at the sight of his mother as a girl. She bit her lip in puzzlement as her gaze took him in from head to toe.

'Nice teeth,' said Alfie. They were pre-SPI teeth, neat and pearly.

'Teeth? What a strange thing to comment on. Are you a Brown?'

Alfie frowned, and looked himself up and down. 'A brown what?'

'A Brown. One of the Brown family.'

'No, I'm a . . .' Janey kicked him before he could say 'Halliday'. 'I'm Alfie, er, Knickers. I'm one of the Knickers family.'

At that Jakobi guffawed, as Maisie Halliday said, 'Strange. Related, maybe.'

Geneva shoved her brother. 'Kobi, there's someone else at the door. Go and get it instead of interfering here.'

'I'll be back,' said Jakobi with a wiggle of his sandy eyebrows.

'Geneva, I need to talk to you,' said Janey, unsure how to start. This was her mother. She'd spent so much of her life lying to her, not able to tell her the truth. No more, she decided. There wasn't time.

'You might want to sit back down again,' she said, just as Rosie Biggenham burst through the door.

'You'd better listen up,' blurted Rosie, 'because it's all completely true and magic! Kobi, you go away.'

'Make me,' said Jakobi, folding his arms and pushing out his biceps.

But when four angry girls turned on him (and Alfie, still suffering from shock), he backed away with a mocking smile. 'You'll be sorry when you need a big strong lad around. I can see Mr Knickers isn't going to be any use to you. But all right, girls, I'll leave you in peace.'

As the door closed behind him, Janey X-rayed until she was sure he'd gone downstairs and then turned to the crowded bedroom. 'I don't know where to start, but here goes . . .'

It took about twenty minutes for her to explain as much as she possibly could to Geneva and Maisie, and to fill in various gaps for Rosie and even for Alfie. To their great credit, nobody stopped her until she said, 'So now Solomon's been carted away, and Boz is really sick, and I *still* have to find my dad as a grown-up, which is why we came here in the first place.'

'This is . . . insane! Surely you don't expect us to believe this?' Maisie bristled with indignation as Geneva gazed at her toes, open-mouthed, shaking her head from time to time.

'I know it sounds crazy,' said Janey. 'But, Geneva, Boz sent me here – he says you're the answer.'

137

'Me?' Geneva stared at her. 'I don't even know Boz. Why would I be the answer?'

Janey frowned. 'You don't know Boz? But you marry him in the future.'

At that Geneva howled with laughter. 'Isn't he still at primary school or something? He must be years younger than me, if he's not even appeared at Everdene yet!'

'I think he's just home-schooled because he's very bright,' Janey suggested.

Geneva shrugged. 'Even more reason! I'm not marrying a nerd!'

'Are you sure you don't mean Solomon?' said Maisie quietly.

'Maisie, how many times – it's not *me* Solomon's interested in,' said Geneva.

'That's right!' Janey grabbed Maisie's hands impulsively. 'You! He likes you. That's why he was hanging around you at the fashion show, and . . .'

Geneva and Maisie both fell around giggling on the floor, but Janey suspected she could hear a note of relief in Maisie's laughter. Alfie, meanwhile, looked ready to throw up.

Geneva turned back to Janey. 'We shouldn't be laughing, but you have to admit it all sounds very far-fetched. Like something on the telly.'

'Prove it to them, Blonde,' said Rosie. 'Put on your Invisibubble. I made these,' she added proudly.

So Janey did a few SPI-buy demonstrations, and by the end both girls looked very sober. 'But why?' asked Geneva. 'Why am I the answer? I don't get it.'

'It's something to do with your name, I think.' Janey pulled a scrap of paper from her pocket and wrote 'GENEVA' on it in the same way Boz had done. 'See, two Es and a V are underlined. It's the same in R-Evolver and BELIEVƎ. Does that mean anything to you? And then there's this symbol we've been seeing everywhere – the backward E with a cross through it.'

Geneva threw up her hands. 'I'm sorry. Nothing. Maybe it's something to do with Switzerland? Geneva's the capital. And there's a cross on the Swiss flag.'

Janey shook her head. 'I don't know. That's all we have. Apart from . . . well, there were these palindrome squares in Sol's den.'

And in two little noughts-and-crosses grids she sketched out the two boxes side by side.

T	E	N
E	V	E
N	E	T

A	N	D
N	A	N
D	N	A

And at the same moment, she and Alfie saw it. Alfie let out a low whistle. 'DNA. Far out.'

'What's that when it's at home?' said Maisie briskly. Janey almost smiled. It was suddenly very clear where Alfie had got his dislike of not being the first to know everything.

He squared his shoulders. 'DNA stands for Deoxyribose Nucleic Acid. It's what our cells are made from, in two strands that twist around like a . . .'

'Helter-skelter,' said Janey slowly. 'Like the BE-LIEVƎ slide.'

'It contains the genetic information about how we're made,' said Alfie, looking rather pleased with himself.

Janey gasped. 'No! Not you, Alfie. I mean, of course, you're made the same way too, but don't you get it? This is all about females. All the names on the BELIEVƎ slide are female! Mum! I mean, Geneva, that's why Boz said you've got the answer. Have . . . have you got a family tree?'

'What, like an . . . oak or something?'

'No, a chart that shows all your family background.'

'Oh!' Geneva looked a trifle embarrassed, then her expression cleared. 'Yes! Grandmere embroidered something like that for me, seeing as how my parents died when I was young. Wait here!'

In seconds she was back with a large picture frame in her hands. She levered it on to the floor and they all dropped to their knees around it. 'There's me,' she said, pointing to her name, which had Jakobi's name next to it and a little line leading up to another pair of names: Monique Delacroix and Andrew Bond. Janey gasped. 'Yes! Monique the Unique Delacroix!'

'Both my parents died in a skiing accident. Rosie's parents were with them at the time. That's why I . . .' She stopped, blushing, but Janey knew what she meant. That's why she looked out for Rosie when nobody else did. Their families went way back. Geneva traced her finger up the line above her mother's name. 'Grandmere brought us up so we use her name. Here she is: Marie Delacroix.'

Janey nodded. 'They're all the names on the BELIEVƎ slide. That's how each generation is listed – by the female. And there's another one.' She grabbed a pen and traced a line to the side of her mother's name and wrote 'Boz Brilliance Brown', and then drew another line down from the pair of them. 'Me,' she said, writing JANE BLONDE on the glass. 'The last one.'

'The last in a long line of spies,' said Alfie thoughtfully. 'It was on your mum's side, not your dad's. Weird.'

They all stared at each other as the implications sunk in. Somehow the BELIEVƎ technology traced their DNA through the mother and twisted it back in time so they could travel through the generations via the double helix of which DNA was formed. No wonder it was making people sick. They were rewriting their very existence.

Alfie tapped the pane of glass carefully. 'So if you're the last one, who's the first? THE MIGHTY EVE?'

'She's so many names back,' said Janey. 'It's impossible to say. Our first ancestor?'

At that Alfie whipped off his PERSPIRE. 'Don't know if this will work here, but let's try . . .' And he tapped 'First Ancestor Eve' into the Google bar as the girls watched, agog. 'Thank goodness your dad's a genius,' he said, pointing at the screen, and then he went white.

Janey followed his finger. 'The most recent common ancestor is known as Mitochondrial Eve. There is no suggestion that Mitochondrial Eve is the same as the Biblical Eve,' she read aloud. 'Living one hundred and forty thousand years ago, she is believed to be the woman from whom all living humans are descended. Scientists have named her Eve.'

'THE MIGHTY EVE!' whispered Rosie reverently.

Janey sat back to let the information sink in. They were all descended from one woman: Eve. 'Oh no,' she whispered, suddenly understanding the B4 EVE message that Boz had given her. 'Dad wants me to go back one hundred and forty thousand years to Eve's time. I can't . . . How will that help? Alfie, what's wrong? Don't worry. I won't do it!'

Alfie was staring at her and then at Maisie. 'This is all about the mothers. What about the fathers?'

So he'd worked it out. Sol's true identity. Alfie swallowed hard. 'Who did I remind you of?' he whispered. 'Who?'

Maisie shrugged. 'I . . . well, I don't like to say really, but you're a lot like . . . a lot like Solomon Brown.'

'And I'm also a lot like . . . Copernicus. My father.'

'I'm sorry, Alfie,' said Janey, but the words just wouldn't stretch to make it any better.

15 ugalee solly b

'He wasn't that bad,' Alfie said, leaning over as if he was going to be sick. 'Young Solomon just wasn't that bad! A bit full of himself, but he couldn't have turned into . . . into something so evil.'

Maisie grabbed hold of Alfie's collar. 'Pull yourself together.'

'All right, Mu-um,' moaned Alfie. 'What's up with you?'

'You all keep talking about Sol as if he's some kind of monster,' said Maisie gruffly. 'Well, he's not. He's my friend. He's very helpful and kind, even though he doesn't like to show it.'

'It makes sense. Even his name,' Jane whispered, thinking aloud. 'Solomon . . . Sol . . . Doesn't that mean "sun" in French or Spanish or something? Copernicus's sun mask!'

Alfie still looked nauseous. 'I can't believe it. So my father wasn't always terrible. He was trying to help little Bozzy. I heard him.'

Everyone jumped as the SPIV around Janey's neck trilled and a dark voice penetrated the room. 'Jane Blonde, I have a hostage. I'll surrender him – but only in exchange for you.'

'It's him!' squeaked Alfie, staring in horror at the SPI Visualator.

Janey felt her heart thump beneath the SPIV. The image on the tiny screen was difficult for them all to see, so she took off her Ultra-gogs, held them in front of the Visualator and commanded the glasses to project.

Solomon Brown's handsome face glowered at her venomously from Geneva's white wardrobe door. 'The Boy-battler,' she whispered. 'The Invisibubble Boy-battler I gave him in the ambulance. He used it to escape. But where did he get the SPIV?'

'Never mind that. I see you can be intelligent when you want to, Blonde,' said Solomon lightly, licking the salty trail of blood across his upper lip. In the future, the gash on his face would get worse and worse with each transformation until he wouldn't be able to stand for it to be seen in public. And then he'd have his sun mask hammered out, until even that wasn't enough and he'd appear in SPIRIT form only. Knowing his fate, and despite all he had done, she felt pity for him.

Until he grabbed a handful of hair and pulled up the face of the person at his feet so that it too could be seen on the screen. 'Boz,' cried Janey. 'Don't! That's my . . .'

'Right again,' said Solomon. 'Your wonderful leader. We'll have you on Pop Quiz soon. Oh. No, we won't. Because you're not going to live.' His voice quavered, and Janey recognized that it wasn't just madness or fury fuelling his words. It was sadness too.

'They were going to send me away, Blonde.' Solomon let Boz's head drop again, but kept hold of the SPIV around Boz's neck so that he dangled from it like a scarecrow losing its stuffing. 'Put me in a mental institution. Fix electrodes to my head. Wipe my memory clean. All because of him.'

'It's not his fault,' cried Janey. 'He's just a boy, and he's sick!'

'I know he's sick.' Venom at the betrayal of his family dripped through every word. 'They all are – the whole family. Lancelot Brown, my ancestor. Ha! – what kind of psychopath has to have a whole village put underwater just so he can build a pretty garden? You see where I get it from . . . where *we* get it from.'

'He's not sick like that, and neither were your ancestors,' said Janey furiously as Alfie put a restraining hand on her arm. 'It's the time travel, and his inventions. They've made him sick.'

'Ah yes, all those marvellous inventions you told me I'd created.' Solomon sighed, a long shuddering sigh that seemed to turn Geneva's bedroom cold. 'I believed you! I suppose I wanted to. Do you know how long I've been sidelined by this brilliant little brother of mine? How long I've played second fiddle while the family simper over him? He's not even at Everdene yet – imagine how much worse it will be when he's in the same school as me and takes over my little head-quarters under the stage. I can't take it. I won't . . . won't take it.'

Maisie jumped forward and shouted awkwardly into Janey's chest. 'Don't do anything silly, Solomon. Please. Some of us . . .' She searched for words. 'Some of us really do appreciate you.'

Solomon's anguished face softened. 'Thanks, Maisie. But I think you're a bit of a lone voice.'

'No, she's not!' shouted someone behind her. Alfie fell forward, scarlet in the cheeks. 'I mean, I don't really know you, and I've never had much time for you so far, but you're not all bad like we thought you were – um, are – and you don't need to do anything you don't want to. But don't hurt that little boy,' he added, seeing Boz slumped at Solomon's leg.

Solomon's burning gaze sought Janey. 'And what about you, Blonde? What do you think of me?'

'I . . . I think . . .'

She couldn't. Couldn't think. Suddenly she was just nervous Janey Brown again. Put on the spot by someone bigger and more powerful. And what *did* she think of him anyway? Standing down a boy not much older than herself, a boy who had as yet done nothing wrong, was miles away from coming face to face with an arch-rival who had carried out countless evil crimes. 'It's just . . .'

Get a hold of yourself, Blonde, she told herself. This was just like it used to be when she tried to stand up to Alfie, the most popular boy in school, and the headmistress's son to boot. And that had worked out all right. She took a deep breath. 'I think you're bluffing,' she said. 'You won't hurt him. He's your brother. You love him.'

'I do?' Solomon threw back his head and laughed. 'I do! You're right. So no, I won't hurt him myself. But I don't need to. He's dying anyway. The squid thing hasn't helped him recover the same way it helped me.'

From behind Geneva, Rosie shouted out: 'That's because the squid is YOU, you idiot! You're sapping strength from yourself, don't you see?'

'Well, at least I'm alive. I'm so alive. I will stay . . . ALIVE.' And Solomon pointed a finger directly at the SPIV screen. 'JB, I won't hurt him. But I will definitely hurt you. Come and fight, if you're spy enough.'

'Where?' screamed Janey, watching in terror as Solomon strode away, dragging her father by the scruff of the neck like a puppy about to be drowned.

Solomon let out a horrible hollow laugh, and Janey saw the split of light and dark as his hand dipped into the R-Evolver time machine. 'Where my sun is rising, Blonde. I'll see you where my sun is rising.'

And they all watched, dismayed, as he dropped the crumpled heap that was Boz Brilliance Brown on the grass and disappeared inside the tractor tyre.

'What does that mean?' Janey spun around, but the others looked as blank as she felt. 'He's going somewhere in the BELIEVƎ. Where's he going?'

Alfie shook himself, trying to clear his head. 'We've got to find him before he . . .' Before he turns into a vile monster, was what Alfie was avoiding saying. 'His sun – the beginning of time?'

Suddenly Janey thought of something. There *was* a place where Solomon was still king. At least for a while. 'Everdene!' she gasped. 'The grandfather clock has a moon on the face.'

'And it's coming up to midnight,' said Geneva, checking her watch, 'so the sun will be rising.'

'I have to go.' Janey sprinted for the door. 'Geneva, Rosie – could you tell your grown-up selves what's going on? Alfie, lend them your SPIV.'

'So you're going to face Sol on your own?' Alfie handed his SPIV to Geneva, nipped around her and stopped Janey at the door. 'I don't think so.'

'I'll be fine, Alfie. And I don't want you to have to fight your own dad.'

Alfie battled with his emotions, then shrugged. 'Tough one that. But maybe if I fight, it will be for his own good – you know, in the future. And anyway, I'm not letting you do this alone.'

'We're coming too,' piped Rosie B, 'because it looks like Sol isn't going to be doing this alone either!'

She pointed to Janey's chest. The SPIV was still screening images from the SPIV around Boz's neck. It was facing upwards, into the trajectory of the dark/light column in the centre of the R-Evolver and they could see all manner of hideous creatures pouring out of the BELIEVƎ slide.

'What on *earth* is that?' Maisie Halliday squinted at the tiny screen, appalled.

'Oh lordy lord lordy,' hissed Rosie. 'Do not like the look of that. Is it a dog? Come 'ere and I'll sit on ya!' she hollered.

Janey and Alfie were the only ones to recognize it. It was the rat-dog that had formed from Copernicus's water-rat supporters when they'd used the Nine-Lives bubble. 'He's gone back and got it!' whispered Janey in horror.

'Forward. Technically he's gone forward and got it,' said Alfie helpfully. 'Oh no – and them too? Euw! Not her!'

'Her' was his half-sister, Paulette, who had terrorized them all with the water rats. Behind her came another small girl, dressed like Goldilocks, a small pistol in her hand, and a bunch of thugs right behind her. Mutated whales and hippos, hordes of gorilla henchmen, and a wild assortment of angry humans – all supporters of Copernicus at some point in time, and all involved in his battles with Jane Blonde – were spurting from the centre of the R-Evolver, diving to the floor, rolling and picking themselves up, forming ranks, marching. Marching. Marching towards the school.

'He's building himself an army,' said Janey, horrified as she watched dozens of Jane Blondes being spat out of the R-Evolver. 'The evil clones! Look, he's got the clones from Dubbo Seven – Alfie, there's you, and Mum, and your mum, and G-Mamma. Oh!' The clone G-Mammas looked so wonderfully well and bubbly that Janey couldn't stand to think of the real version, wasting away in the future.

She grabbed Alfie's SPIV from Geneva's hands. 'G-Mamma! He's bringing everyone. Everyone from the past! I mean . . . the . . . the future, his future. We need back-up! Please send Bert, and Tish and Magenta, and the Birds, and even Leaf and his dad . . .'

'Me too!' croaked G-Mamma.

'No!' Janey raced for the bedroom door, skidding on a stray marble and almost catapulting herself down the stairs, barely stopping to right herself as she sprang down them, waving to the others to follow. 'You've got the sickness. It's because of the DNA sharing from the BELIEVƎ machine. That's why Copernicus is nearly dead – he's here, and Solomon's getting stronger and stronger, as if he's sapping the cells from his future self. Rosie will do the same to you. If you come back, you'll die! And the same applies to Mum, and Mrs Halliday. You mustn't meet yourselves. You can't!'

'Oh, all right then,' huffed G-Mamma. 'SPIV me later then.'

'I will. G-Mamma, I . . . tell Mum . . . I'm sorry. I messed up. I love you both, and Dad, and it's all gone wrong . . .'

But the SPIV had gone dead. And if she let the horrible tingling across her nose take hold and make her cry, like she really, really wanted to, then the SPIV wouldn't be the only thing that was dead. Jane Blonde had to move – fast. Everyone else was in the car already, so she leaped into the passenger seat and smacked the dashboard. 'Floor it,' she screamed.

'Thought you'd never ask,' said Alfie.

16 rats live on no evil star

They raced straight to the school, scouring through the gravel as the car spun to a stop outside the main doors.

'Head for the hall!' shouted Janey. Skirting the grandfather clock, she pointed through the double doors at the stage. 'Up. Keep *up*. As high as you can.'

'Sorry. Bit of a detour!' cried Rosie, running past Janey towards the back of the school.

'Rosie, no, we need you . . . Come back!'

But the girl's back was disappearing into the distance. Janey swallowed a sigh. Terrified, and you could hardly blame her. So that left a total of two Spylets and two untrained amateurs. How were they going to survive against a whole squadron – several squadrons – of evil doers? But they couldn't give up. The hubbub from the hall was growing, and suddenly Janey heard a mad howl from its depths.

'Ha! Not here. I knew she wouldn't have the nerve. No girl would have the nerve to face me!'

No girl? She wasn't having that. No way. Reaching for her SPI-Pod, Janey turned up the MIC facility and spoke into it. 'I'm here, Solomon. Right outside.'

'Outside?' The voice that replied sounded confused, caught between excitement and disappointment. There was more of the young Solomon in Copernicus than Janey had really thought. Perhaps . . . Perhaps they wouldn't need to battle it out at all. 'Stand the troops down, Solomon,' she called. 'This has got out of hand. We don't need to fight. Let me put it right.'

Suddenly a terrifying sight appeared at the glass panes in the large school doors. A mask. Jagged and huge. Shaped like the sun, but with none of its warmth, like a demented, evil sunflower. Copernicus's mask. From its centre two dark, intense eyes glared at her. 'Look what I found,' hissed Solomon.

'That's not you,' said Janey as Alfie, Maisie and Geneva moved in behind her, protecting her back and sides with whatever they'd had chance to grab from Geneva's house – one framed family history, a roller skate and a pillow. 'You don't have to become that. You can choose to be someone different.'

'Too . . . LATE.'

Solomon threw open the doors, and the whirling masses in the hall behind him turned as one. Then the room fell apart in uproar, squeals and howls of rage from mink and rats and mutated hippos, thumping war dances from Paulette and the Sinerlesse members, and a massive chant rising from the ranks . . .

'We'll thrash 'em.
We'll bash 'em . . .'

'. . . We'll round them up and mash 'em,' repeated Geneva, listening to the terrifying cries of the G-Mamma clones within. 'Is that us they're talking about?'

'Yes, I'm sorry to say,' said Janey. 'We can run, or we can fight.'

'Fight,' said Geneva, and placed her hand on Janey's shoulder. 'Maisie, you?'

'Fight,' agreed Maisie, laying her hand on top of Geneva's. 'But only to save Solomon from himself.'

'Same,' said Alfie, adding his hand to the pile. It wasn't clear whether he meant he just wanted to fight, or he wanted to save Solomon, but now was not the time to ask. They all stared for a second at their linked fingers, then Janey pushed them all down. They were a team. 'You are all the most amazing spies. I wish we had more help, but we have to start somewhere. Let's go.'

They turned in unison towards the open double doors, where a mocking Solomon stood like an evil cinema usher. 'We have to get past him first,' said Janey.

'Leave him to me,' said Maisie, and she strode forward, holding the embroidery out in front of her like a shield. 'Solomon Brown. Do you know what this is? It's a family tree: mums and dads and daughters and sons. And one day we'll have one of these of our own.'

The information caught Solomon off guard; he didn't move but was still staring at the picture frame as Maisie marched up, pulled the Sun King mask away from his face and planted a huge kiss directly on his scarred lips. The mask clattered to the floor as Solomon touched his mouth in disbelief. 'What was that for?' he said.

Maisie rolled her eyes. 'What do you think?'

Alfie was gagging next to Janey. 'That is so disgusting.'

'It's a life-or-death moment,' said Janey, and she looked sideways at her friend. 'Doesn't it make you want to kiss me?'

At which Alfie turned deathly pale. 'Euw! Sicko! I mean, love you lots and all that, Blonde, but not . . . no, thanks!' He made hacking noises like a cat about to cough up a hairball.

Janey laughed. He was absolutely right – and she loved him lots too. He was her very best friend, after all. 'OK. Well, let's hope your mum . . . oh.'

They turned again to see Maisie pinned up against the door frame, a jagged metal edge point skewering the skin across her throat. Solomon was leaning over her, the dagger-like sun mask perilously close to Maisie's jugular veins. 'You feel sorry for me! Sorry! That's all – pity for the mad boy. For the poor son who'll amount to nothing next to the genius, Bowood. I will not have people feeling sorry for me any longer. Do you hear me?'

'I d-d- . . . I don't . . .'

But Alfie had had enough. 'Get off my mother, you monster!' With a bang of his Fleet-feet against the floor, the boy Spylet blasted along the corridor towards the hall, wiping out a pair of Janey clones who were heading towards them and pelting straight between Solomon and Maisie with an elbow to Solomon's chest.

'Alfie, be careful, he's got the Battler!' shouted Janey, running after them and hauling Geneva along beside her at Fleet-feet speed. But her warning came too late; Solomon curled his fist and Janey knew that, even though they couldn't see it, the Boy-battler on his right hand would be doubling, trebling in size, gaining in weight till it was as solid and heavy as a wrecking ball. With a furious roar, he whammed his arm around and smacked Alfie in the back of the head. The Spylet took off from the impact, sailing straight into the hall, right into the centre of the enemy crowds.

157

'Come on!' Janey screamed to Maisie, who was reeling in the doorway. She thrust the Sun King mask into her hands to fight with, before pulling off her Girl-gauntlet and handing it to Geneva. 'No time to explain – just whack people and squeeze the fingers and something will happen!' She smoothed her own Jane Blonde ponytail. It was pretty much the only weapon she still had. If only they'd had time to re-Wow. To go back for help. To see everyone one last time . . .

But Alfie was struggling in the middle of the room, trying to hold his own as water rats and a bevy of Gina-clones kicked and slashed at him, and G-Mammas rapped. He was on his knees, protecting his head, doing what he could to lash out with his coiled SuSPInder, but the crowds were too thick for it to have much impact.

'Maisie, Geneva, throw me!' yelled Janey.

The two girls looked at each other, perplexed, but then turned with their hands linked in front of them as if they'd rehearsed the move. Socking a Mrs Halliday-clone with her foot as she jumped, Jane Blonde bounced straight up to them, rammed a foot into each pair of joined hands, and was launched into the air above the melee. Up she flew, checking for Alfie, scanning for something suitable to land on. She only had seconds, fractions of seconds, but in that time she managed to pull SPInamite from her suit, chew on it three times and lob it out into the far reaches of the hall where the gathering clones were surging forward from the den under the stage, desperate for their turn to fight, test their mettle. A dozen fake Alfies stared up as the gum arced down towards them, and then scattered as it hit the ground, sending a shower of sparks and splinters from the hall floor and scraps of fake-Alfie-SPIsuit into the air like a fountain.

She was coming down now, head first, a swallow dive that might well end in tragedy. 'Turn, Blonde,' grunted Janey, and she closed herself up into a tight ball so that she somersaulted one and half times. Better. Now she was feet first. Still too far from Alfie to help – and from the air she could see how much he needed it – but heading in the right direction at least. And there was her enemy – tall, upright, hardly able to believe his luck that his nemesis was going to land right in front of him.

Or so he thought. Janey had other plans. 'Nice broad shoulders,' she thought as she plummeted towards Solomon. He took a step backwards; she adjusted her angle, and suddenly her feet landed heavily on either side of his neck. He went to grab them, but found himself screaming in pain as Jane Blonde's Fleet-feet detonated, showering sparks into his face which was no longer protected by his sun mask, which was in fact being used by Maisie, partly as a shield, partly as a fearful spinning, chopping wheel to fend off enemy spies. Solomon's shoulders slumped as the full force of the Fleet-feet jump impacted on them, and suddenly Janey was sailing above the heads of the crowd again.

Not a moment too soon. Alfie was crouched on the floor, unable to defend himself in any way other than to protect his head with his hands, which were bloodied and gashed from the continuing onslaught of the enemies around him. As she fell towards him, Janey threw out her arms and legs and made contact with as many clones and mutated creatures as she possibly could, even spinning on the spot and whipping her ponytail into the eyes of a host of Gina Bellarinas so that they staggered back, tears of agony pouring down their faces.

'Agent Halo, I'm right behind you,' she said, shoving SPInamite into her mouth. 'Spin me round!'

'Right, like I'm supposed to believe you're the *real* one,' he moaned. Janey could see what he meant – he was surrounded by Blonde-clones every bit as eager to kill him as she was to save him. How to prove her true identity?

'It's just like a game of football,' she said hurriedly. 'I've set up the goal; now you're going to score. Only hurry up, because otherwise my head will blow off.'

'Football?' Alfie got to his feet, fending off a G-Mamma and an advancing whale with hippo legs. 'Only the real Jane Blonde would know that's nearly as important to me as spying. But spin you round – why?'

'Trust me!' squeaked Janey, screwing up her eyes. If he didn't do something immediately, they'd both die anyway. 'And then duck!'

So Alfie grabbed her by the shoulders and spun her clockwise, then dropped to a crouch. Janey's Fleet-feet whizzed, turning her round like a dervish, just like her eSPIdrills had done when they had bored through the planet to Australia, and all the blobs of SPInamite that she'd busily planted in her ponytail sprayed out across the room, falling in a shower of explosions that wiped out entire pockets of enemies near and far.

It wasn't enough though.

'Blonde!' Someone screamed, and Janey turned to see Geneva, horrified, holding up her fist to fight but completely encircled by a score or more of her own future self. Gina Bellarinas were advancing, kicking out, their burnished helmets of hair blinding in the bright school lights of the hall.

'Go!' yelled Alfie, pushing her through a narrow corridor that the SPInamite blasts had created. 'I'll help Mum. You go!'

Geneva was now swiping helplessly at the marauding Gina Bellarinas with the pillow, saying, 'Pillow fight! Go on, laugh. That was funny,' but she didn't sound in the least bit amused. She sounded petrified. But then Janey noticed the way the lights were held up. 'Geneva! Third finger!' she hollered, pointing to the cable from which the lights swung above their heads.

She ran forward, elbowing Bellarinas out of the way to give Geneva time to act. 'Ha!' shouted Geneva as the titanium blade shot out of one finger and ink squirted from another, directly into the open mouth of an advancing clone.

'I said *third* finger! Point the laser!' Janey gestured above their heads. Grabbing her Ultra-gogs, she waved them in the air until the laser found them and shot through, magnified in force a hundred times or more. Less than a second later, the cable supporting the central set of lights down the middle of the hall had burned through completely; the great fluorescent strip lights lashed down like a twenty-metre cat-o'-nine-tails, a storm of glass and lights and cable cutting a great swathe through the enemy ranks.

Geneva whooped joyfully.

Janey paused just long enough to glance around. 'But there're still only four of us and dozens of them.'

Geneva stared bleakly at her, then looked around. Maisie was backing up against her, forced to retreat by a viciously snarling rat-dog that was more than a match for the razor-like Sun King mask. Alfie lay on his back nearby. For a moment Janey thought he'd been killed. He was so still . . . but then she saw his hand creep furtively across the floor, snaking through the stamping feet of the enemy army, and then just as the rat-dog got dangerously close to Maisie's foot, he pushed a stray roller skate into its path.

'Trust Alfie to find a vehicle,' Janey cried, pointing it out to Geneva. It travelled under the feet of the rat-dog so that it flailed helplessly, suddenly looking ridiculous rather than scary, and then across the toes of a platoon of clone Janey Browns. Wimpy as they were, they all stared down at their feet at once and burst into tears.

'Who are they?' said Geneva in disgust. '*What* are they?'

'You don't want to know. Come on.' Janey and Alfie looked around for an escape route, dragging Maisie along by one of the points of the mask.

But as she assessed their situation, Janey's heart sank. They were completely surrounded. Granted, some of the bodies in the circle around them were on the floor, possibly dead or injured or passed out, but the other enemy creatures and human-types were clambering over them anyway, not even stopping to check injuries or to answer the pitiful cries of the dying.

'It's no good,' said Janey, feeling the tug of horrified tears behind her eyes. Not tears for herself. She didn't worry for herself any more. But for Alfie and Maisie and Geneva and the people she loved in the future. Even for Solomon, who was

163

driving troops forward from the back, standing at the entrance to the den, his dark eyes searching for her, to seek and destroy. As she looked back she thought she saw another pair of eyes nearby. Pale, vivid and blue. Bluer than her father's. Anyway, by now they had disappeared, and she shook her head.

'I'm sorry, everyone. This is never going to work. Not without a miracle anyway.'

But just as she wondered how to tell them to get out as best they could, the miracle appeared. And she was on the stage, back-lit, in full make-up.

17 battler battles

Music thumped from the same tinny cassette player that had played during the fashion show. All heads turned towards the stage as the lights that hadn't come down in the laser attack dimmed, on cue from a sparkling fingernail. And then the platform that started in the den beneath the stage rose up from the depths. On it was a goddess, a vision in shimmering sapphire silk, with gossamer batwings that she held up above her head so they fanned out like an angel's.

'It is a miracle,' whispered Janey.

'Miracle? It's Rosie Biggenham, for crying out loud,' said Maisie in astonishment.

BANG! A spotlight centred on the stage. The tape fell silent. The ranks of enemy spies were spellbound as Rosie B stepped forward from her platform, a SPI-Pod microphone strapped to her cheek with masking tape. 'Rosie B's in the house,' she said quietly.

She had no need to shout. You could have heard a pin drop.

But then the music was turned up and, to Janey's amazement, as Rosie moved to the front of the stage, a trio of backing singers walked in from the wings. One. Two. Three. Mrs Halliday, in a gleaming red boiler suit. Gina Bellarina, in a tight bronze SPIsuit. And lastly, hobbled over, a shadow of her former self, but smiling bravely and broadly through her sparkly make-up, enveloped by a vast purple ballgown, was G-Mamma. The music burst into a crescendo, and all three raised their right arm, then pointed at Rosie Biggenham. 'Spylets are forevaghghghgh!' she screamed.

'Oh. It's horrible. Horrible horrible.' Alfie stared at the girl at his side, back at his mother on the stage, and then back at Maisie, who was starting to squint at the older version of herself on the stage with a very suspicious expression. 'That looks like my grandmother up there . . .'

'Never mind that,' gasped Janey. 'Look at the effect their singing is having on Copernicus's army!' Clones, animals and Spylets were paralysed, staring vacantly at the stage.

'Spylets are forevahhhhhh!' hollered Rosie B, catching Janey's eye, and beckoning her forward, she lobbed a flurry of articles in her direction. Janey handed them out as Maisie and Geneva continued to stare. Gauntlets. Boy-battlers. SuSPInders. Replacement

Fleet-feet. A Back-boat. All the gadgets, it seemed, that G-Mamma had sent Rosie back with when she visited. That was why she'd left the hall. To get help. Rally the troops. And do her job of providing gadgets, even if it wasn't her job yet.

Behind Rosie, G-Mamma tried to smile at Janey and stuck her wizened thumb in the air. She could barely manage even that.

'That one in the bronze should know better!' said Geneva in disgust. 'She's completely too old to wear anything that tight. And that stupid short haircut. Who are these people?'

Taking a deep breath, Janey prepared to introduce the SPIs to themselves, but at that moment she realized three things.

One, the enemy was stirring again.

Two, a small troop was joining the four on the stage, and that was why the enemy were getting restless. Hardly surprising when the extras consisted of Agent Dubbo Seven, Agent Titian and her mother Magenta, the Erikssens (former double agent Leaf and his father) and a whole family in shimmering black SPIsuits.

Three, the worst realization by far: she'd been delighted to see them, but the reason she had told the three backing singers to stay away still existed. They couldn't meet themselves as youngsters, or they'd become ill. As if to prove the point, G-Mamma suddenly doubled over and staggered to her knees. Rosie stopped yelling mid-sentence and spun around to help her, and as her fingers touched G-Mamma's shoulders the SPI:KE collapsed completely, sprawling over the stage in a puddle of purple silk.

It was time to fight again. Rosie had done a brilliant job, but the enemy had had enough now; many were back on their feet, looking venomously at the stage.

'Fall back,' said Janey under her breath. 'Geneva, Maisie, you have to fight at the rear. Don't join up with the women on the stage, whatever you do.'

Alfie nodded. 'You're in defence. Blonde and I will cover the midfield, and that lot on the stage,' he whispered, 'are the attack.'

'Don't go all superior and footbally on me,' said Maisie. 'I'm in the County Girls Eleven, I'll have you know.'

So that was where he got it from! Janey gave Geneva a gentle shove and pulled on a new Girl-gauntlet. Rosie Biggenham screamed, 'SPY-PETS!' and Janey gasped at the brilliant sight of a cawing pterodactyl sweeping the room, and Maddy the spy-sheep floating over their heads with a Wowed and glorious Trouble on her back. An evil dachshund rushed from the back of the enemy ranks and tried in vain to snap at Maddy's little cloven hooves. 'Put your hats on!' warned Jane as Maddy responded with a machine-gun volley of poo pellets, and Trouble waggled his sabre claw menacingly, his emerald eyes sweeping the room like the beam from a lighthouse.

The tide was turning. As Trouble let out a victorious yowl, SPIs leaped and swung and bounced from the stage like a circus troupe, attacking, swinging at anyone who got in their way. True to their position, Geneva and Maisie stationed themselves at the back of the hall, a SuSPInder stretched between them. Every time Tish or Raven or one of their allies surged forward, the girls at the back held firm and pushed back with the SuSPInder. Jane Blonde and Al Halo Battled and Gauntleted and ponytailed, the force field which was created from the spy ring and surrounded them, allowing them to knock others into oblivion while being completely protected themselves.

From the stage, Rosie B directed operations via the SPI-Pod MIC, all the while holding on to G-Mamma. 'Mrs H, behind you! Sock it to 'em, baby! Yeah! Now watch out. Ten o'clock – incoming enemies. Get 'em, Gina Bellarina! Oooooooo, nice drop kick! OK – little person in black shimmery stuff . . . whatever your name is!' She leaned down to G-Mamma. 'Oh, right – Blackbird. Oi, Blackbird! Give that nasty little doggywoggy a peck on the tail. Bad dachshund! Silly sausage!'

Janey drew up next to Alfie, shoulder to shoulder under the force field. 'I think we're winning!'

Alfie pointed his ring finger upwards so the

169

force field lifted, then sent a projectile of SPInamite attached to the roller skate out into the crowd. A flash of pale blue streaked along at eye level, then the middle of the floor disappeared with a resounding *thwump*, taking with it a phalanx of hippos being ridden by Freda, Miss Lear and various other Sinerlesse members.

'Blonde, I was just wondering . . .' Alfie grabbed a G-Mamma clone by the nose, yanked hard, and then cast her off to one side, howling in agony.

'What?' said Janey, running up the inside of the force field and across the top, upside down, so her feet knocked off all the horrible creatures swarming all over it.

Alfie paused. 'I just haven't seen Solomon for a while.'

'You're right.' Back on the ground, Janey stopped short. She'd forgotten about him.

But he hadn't forgotten them. That became horribly clear as a familiar voice spoke into the SPI-Pod microphone. 'Not over till the fat girl sings, eh, Biggenham?'

Janey whipped around. Solomon had ripped the mike from Rosie's face and she crouched at his feet, protecting G-Mamma as best she could. 'St-st-sticks and st-stones may break my b-bones . . .' she said bravely, but Solomon didn't even speak – he simply wedged his foot in her side and rocked Rosie and G-Mamma off the stage and on to the floor.

The dark eyes searched the crowd and found what they were looking for. With a peculiar half-smile, made all the more distinctive by the globule of blood oozing down his lip from his barely sealed gash, Solomon beckoned to someone behind the curtains. A broken, shuddering body in blue pyjamas dragged itself out on to the stage.

'Jane Blonde,' said Solomon softly, and for the first time Janey could hear the deep venom that would always pierce through Copernicus's voice. 'We've seen enough. Now it's time to cut to the chase. With what I've discovered I can pass myself off as little Bozzy here, and nobody will ever know.'

'What . . . what do you mean?' Janey signalled to Alfie to let down the force field, and she walked through the crowd , which parted to let her through, mesmerized by what was going on at the front of the hall.

Solomon smiled again, wincing slightly as the fresh wound on his upper lip opened up again. 'Well, just how many ways can I pretend to be my brother? Crystal Clarification. Hm, maybe. Looks a bit painful. SPIRIT. Perhaps. Difficult to have much impact. Spy-clone. I can make millions of Bowoods. Plant them all over the place. Or . . . I can just kill him now – and take his place.'

Janey had reached G-Mamma. She took hold of the shrunken fingers and looked up at the sneering Solomon.

Solomon stared with a strange, blank expression at his sick brother. Boz looked a little less sick, and despite his eyes being sunken and bloodshot, they were somehow soft and sparkly at the same time. He was staring towards the back of the room, towards Geneva. She was looking back too, and even across the hall, across time, Janey could feel that two souls were meeting for the first time.

'Why would you do that?' she said to Solomon, playing for time. If she could keep him talking . . .

But time had already played out. 'Because of what I discover in the future.' Solomon clapped a hand to Boz's shoulder. 'Because taking over – denying the very existence of a brother – well, that's what darling genius Boz does, isn't it? To me.'

And Janey felt sick to her marrow. What he said was technically correct, although she couldn't believe it, not when she looked into Boz's haunted blue eyes, reddened, love-struck and . . . wise, somehow. No. She didn't want to believe it.

Boz's eyes were on her now. He looked stronger, definitely. But not strong enough. He couldn't even speak to defend himself.

She would have to do it for him. Janey stared deeply into Boz's face, willing her father-to-be to help her. What should I do? She repeated it over and over in her head. *Help me, Dad. What should I do?*

He collapsed, sinking further towards the floor,

weakening again. But his eyes never left her face, until suddenly they flicked down towards the floor. His hand, which had been balled up in a fist, slowly uncurled.

And Janey knew what he was saying, without even having to read the message on his hand.

She had to go back in time. Way, way back.

B4 EVE.

18 the mighty eve

Janey's immediate challenge was working out how to leave without looking as though she was abandoning her friends, and even her family. G-Mamma was pooled at her feet, groaning gently; Janey hardly dared to think it, but her beloved SPI:KE looked close to death. Rosie appeared quite healthy now, but she was too distraught over the state of her future self to make much sense.

Suddenly Janey felt a hand on her shoulder. 'Mum!' She hugged her lovely adult mother tightly, but Solomon was dragging Boz across the stage towards her. 'I've got to go. Get everyone under a spy-ring force field.'

'Let me go instead,' whispered Gina Bellarina, but Janey kissed her cheek and pulled away quickly.

'It has to be me.' She didn't know why yet, but she knew that was the truth. Janey spun around, searching for Alfie. He was running towards her, blasting enemies out of the way with his Boy-battler. 'Alfie, look after everyone.'

'Where are you . . . ?'

There wasn't time to explain. With a quick jump on the spot, Janey launched herself off the hall floor with her Fleet-feet and vaulted the heads of the SPI members surrounding her as she headed for the stage. Straight over the head of Solomon she flew, coming down to land lightly on the platform on which Rosie B had risen up to the stage. Janey faced the crowd for one last time, fighting back tears as she gazed at her friends. 'EMOC!' she shouted, with her hand across her heart, pointing to herself, trying not to see that her mother was crying, that Alfie was staring at her as if she was tearing out his insides, that Boz the boy and the near-death G-Mamma had both lifted their heavy heads to watch her leaving, knowing they might never see her again. Leaving them. Leaving them dying. 'I'll EMOC!'

If only she could know for sure. One hundred and forty thousand years was a very long way to go. As a sob finally erupted from her throat, Jane Blonde triggered the platform mechanism and disappeared beneath the stage.

There was a stray ASPIC on the desk; Janey grabbed it and kicked off down the secret corridor. 'Quicker,' she urged it, pushing herself on, speeding around bends and up inclines. The cellar end of the tunnel was in sight, and this was not the occasion for worrying about her bewildered grandparents. She chomped hard on a chunk of SPInamite and thrust it at the cellar door the instant she emerged from the earth, silver and fluid as a jet of water. The door blew apart and Janey whizzed through, not even slowing as the ASPIC shot across the Browns' yard, up the other side, down the other side and across the field towards the tractor tyre.

'Argh! No Invisibubble!' was her horror-stricken realization as she watched her Girl-gauntlet disappear inside the spinning R-Evolver. She wasn't even sure where they'd left the special suits – somewhere around Geneva's house was all she could remember. Just how sick was she going to feel? There was no telling whether she'd even survive the journey.

But she couldn't let that stop her. There were other sick people – dying people – who meant the world to her, for whom she would risk anything. Everything. 'Here goes,' she said, and Jane Blonde hoisted herself up on to the R-Evolver, smacking the first name on the R-Evolving keypad, and threw herself headlong into the BELIEVƎ slide, heading towards the woman herself – THE MIGHTY EVE.

How long she hurtled down the helter-skelter helix, Janey would never know. She understood though that it made no difference. Her father's creation distorted time so much that the journey she was making could not be measured in those terms, or in any of the usual ways that travel would be described. What was it – miles? Kilometres? Years and decades and centuries and millennia? It was all of those and more, and yet somehow nothing, and suddenly Janey understood how the column that appeared in the R-Evolver appeared as a black void and searing light at the same moment. It was everything and nothing combined, captured by the brilliant mind of her father into a living entity all its own. Maybe that's what we all are, thought Janey, trying to press the acupressure point on her wrist to stop the sick feeling taking over as she blasted and swirled through the BELIEVƎ. Everything and nothing, all at the same time. Everything to the people and things and time around us, but nothing in the greater universe, in the whole great span of time . . . A palindrome. The same backwards and forwards, no matter what anyone tried to change.

A horrible buzzing band was tightening around her temples, and Janey couldn't think any more. This was worse, far worse, than any Satispying she had ever done; it wasn't just her cells that were splitting down, but the contents of her cells, the very elements that made her a person. 'I'm turning into nothing,' she mumbled, just before she passed out.

But then the darkness erupted into light and Janey squirted head first out of a pool of icy water, curving through the air, shedding shimmering droplets in an arc like a leaping silvery salmon. She plunged back into the pool and gasped, coughing water, coming to instantly with the shock of her arrival, just about gathering her thoughts enough to fumble for her SPIder, chewing down on the rubbery gadget so that its legs pinched her nose shut and injected oxygen into her lungs. Relaxing, Janey peered upwards towards the glint of sunlight and kicked for the surface.

She popped her head up and trod water as she took in her surroundings. 'Wow.' She was in the middle of a large body of water, not a lake, but bigger than a pond. A creature she couldn't even begin to name was lapping at the water's edge; behind it was one of its young, nudging for attention, and then, as a backdrop, there was forest. Endless forest. Trees spreading as far as Janey could see in every direction. She shook droplets off her Ultra-gogs and issued her instruction: 'Find . . .' What, exactly? Eve? Would she even be a woman that Janey would recognize as such? '. . . erm . . . human life,' she said uncertainly.

She trod water and scanned the horizon. After a short time the Ultra-gogs let out a tiny beep, then projected an image on to her lens.

The woman was right there! At the water's edge, one hand shielding her deep-set eyes as she gazed out across the pool, searching for something, the other resting on the swollen belly that protruded from the animal skins she had tied around her. 'Eve,' whispered Janey, even though she knew that probably wasn't her real name, if she had a name at all.

Eve turned her head, and Janey gasped. She had a ponytail! Her thick, coarse hair was gathered up in a knot at the back and plastered in mud. Sun protection, guessed Janey. But then Eve moved again, and Janey found herself staring straight into her solemn brown eyes. 'Me! She's looking at me.'

It wasn't surprising really. Jane Blonde had just shot out of the pool like a human rocket. But Eve's posture was relaxed; she looked curious, not scared at all, so Janey swam slowly towards her.

Eve stepped back as Janey approached. She cast her eyes up and down the Spylet's body. She touched her muddy ponytail in wonderment, and Janey smiled, getting hold of the end of her own and showing it to Eve. She was on her own. Behind her was a small shack made of branches and leaves, with a pile of reeds on the ground like the sheaf at Eve's feet.

Janey smiled again, leaning over and cautiously picking up the bundle of reeds. 'You're having a baby,' she said softly, watching for Eve's reaction. 'Shouldn't be carrying stuff.'

Eve just cocked her head and followed as Janey added the reeds to the pile in the shack, then she opened her mouth and grunted from the back of her throat, rubbing her belly.

Somehow Janey understood. 'It's for the baby! You're going to have it soon.'

The woman spread both hands over her stomach. Yes, baby, she seemed to say. Then she touched Janey's ponytail and stared at her eyes, startled by the colour. 'Grey,' said Janey, lifting her eyebrows. She pointed to Eve's eyes. 'Brown.'

Eve lifted a gnarled finger to her lips, mimicking Janey's moving mouth but making no sound. She couldn't talk. How was she going to give Janey the answer to her puzzle? How could Janey's coming here save her father and G-Mamma and all the others?

'This baby,' said Janey, 'I think it's very, very important. You have this baby and then more, and somehow you start a whole . . . well, a whole planet really. A whole human race. Wow. Copernicus would be really jealous.'

And as Janey thought of Solomon, and what he would turn into, she almost passed out again.

Creation. That was the answer. Mitochondrial Eve was here at the beginning of time for the human race, and scientists believed that everyone was descended from her at some point. And that was what Copernicus wanted above all – to create his own planet, a new race of people – people who were loyal to him, and served him. He'd been betrayed, let down by the people who should have loved him – his family – so he'd shrivelled within himself, stopped being human, stopped caring and started searching. For revenge, certainly. But for more than that. For friends.

Janey knew just how that felt, and her stomach twisted in a painful knot as she remembered how much she'd longed for friends, for a bigger family, just as Solomon must have done.

'Oh no.' Janey sank to the floor, Eve clucking over her, concerned. 'It's worse than that. Way, way worse.'

Because it wasn't just that Solomon had *become* that way. He'd been created. Someone had forced his hand, turned him into what he would be. And that person was . . .

'Me,' Janey whispered. 'I did it. I've created . . . everything!' Images flew before her eyes. 'Rosie – she was shy and nervous, and I sent her out there with gadgets and clothes and attitude. I turned her into G-Mamma!' she explained to a bewildered Eve. 'And Mum and Dad, they hadn't even met before tonight – well, that night. But I got them together! And . . . and Solomon loved his brother, he was doing everything he could to save him, even travelling through time and doing whatever Boz said even though Boz outshone him in everything. But then I showed him the future. I took him round and showed him all the things he would destroy and ruin and turn black. I even . . .' Janey swallowed back a sob. 'I even showed him that he'd turn into a squid. Oh, Eve.'

Janey took hold of Eve's hand, her eyes swimming. 'Would you still do it, have this baby, if you knew what you were going to make? We do some terrible things.'

Eve touched Janey's face gently, then rubbed her belly again, calm, steady. Ready for new life. 'Of course you would,' said Janey, finally working out the answer. Family. Eve was starting her family. Nothing would change that. But Eve was tugging at her hand. She led Janey behind the shack and pointed to a large rock.

Someone had scrawled on it with a blackened stick. A picture – a girl with a ponytail. Her initials – JB. And something else. It was that symbol again. The one on Bob's tail. The one on the floor of the Browns' cellar. The one that someone had added to the rebus. It had been a message for her.

The sign for 'there exists', scored through with an X. Janey shook her head. It was so obvious. 'Get my messages?' Jakobi had said. Somehow he'd realized what she'd been doing and he'd been trying to discourage her. To protect his friend Solomon, and his friend's brother, and the whole of humanity. Stop them existing, Jane Blonde. Stop it before it starts.

'B4 EV∃!' Janey whispered. And that was what Boz had meant. Not before time began, but before time began *for them*. Before he invented the time machine, and Jane Blonde went back through the decades to tip everything on its head.

Well, if Jane Blonde had made the mess, Jane

Blonde could clear it up. Whatever she'd created, she could un-create. The only question was how.

'I've got one hundred and forty thousand years to work it out,' said Janey. She grabbed Eve and kissed her grimy cheek, startled as Eve pressed something into her hand. 'Good luck with that human race,' she added, slipping the object inside her pocket. It was a Spyclops, bright blue and covered in sand. She smiled. And then she Fleet-feet dived into the pool and struck out for the whirlpool in the centre.

19 b4 ev9

First she raced back to her own time minus a few days, stopping only long enough to grab a startled and healthy-looking G-Mamma by the shoulders and yell, 'When you send Rosie back with gadgets, make sure she gets everything. EVERYTHING! And she has to install it all.' Then she tipped herself back into the BELIEVƎ machine.

Janey staggered from the tractor tyre, wet, bedraggled, half delirious with the journey and the discoveries she had made. Just about managing to keep herself upright, she stumbled on to the ASPIC that still lay in the grass where it had dropped from her feet and pointed it towards the Brown house. The quickest way back to Everdene was through the cellar tunnel.

She raced through the blown-up trapdoor, only to find Lancelot and Carmel Brown standing in the cellar, examining the damage. 'But that's an enormous hole. And the bang! It must have given Bob such a shock . . .

oh!' Janey's grandmother almost dropped the tortoise.

Lancelot frowned down at Janey. 'Young lady, are you one of Solomon's friends? Were you involved in this wanton vandalism?'

'We don't need any more trouble. Sol has gone away, and we've a very poorly son upstairs, you know,' said Carmel, putting Bob back in his box.

'He's not upstairs,' said Janey quickly.

'Rubbish! Of course Boz is upstairs – he was too sick to move.'

'Not any more. Once he got to school he started to look better.'

Her grandmother fumbled behind her for a rake. 'School? You must be insane. Lancelot, obviously there's no truth in this nonsense, but would you please go and check on Bowood now? Young lady, I think you'd better go.'

'No!' shouted Janey, so determinedly that Carmel dropped the rake. 'I've only just realized – it all makes sense now! My dad must have been here all along – my grown-up dad! That's how Boz knew about the BELIEVƎ machine and all the gadgets, and the den under the stairs. He must have met his older self: old Boz.'

'I don't know who your father is, but I can assure you there is no old Boz,' said Carmel in a slow, calm voice, backing away as if Janey was a rabid dog.

'Yes, there is.' Janey gasped as she remembered

the odd way young Boz kept talking towards his knees or the pillow. 'And I know where he is!'

Carmel picked up the rake again and brandished it at Janey as she scrambled for the cellar stairs. 'No you don't! I'll prod you! I'm very handy with garden utensils.'

Janey sighed and pointed a Gauntleted finger at Carmel. 'Nana, please don't make me zap you with stun gas. I've done enough damage to this family already. Just nod when I speak. Do you want to save Boz?' Carmel hesitated, then nodded shakily. 'And would you prefer that Solomon wasn't so . . . disturbed?' Another nod. 'And would you do anything to protect your family?' This time there was a very firm nod, accompanied by a suspicious squint.

Janey nodded in return. 'So would I.' And she squirted her with the stun gas anyway. 'Sorry, Nana,' she said as she caught her grandmother's slight frame and eased her to the floor.

She ran past the lounge, where Lancelot was on the phone, screaming about abduction and missing sons and the state of the world today. While he was distracted she locked the door and pocketed the key, then took the stairs two at a time, carrying the ASPIC above her head. First she skidded to Solomon/Alfie's room. The inert figure of Copernicus still lay on the bed, although now he was tied down with what looked like a garden hose. Only the flicker of his human eyelid showed that he might still be alive. 'I'll EMOC,' shouted Janey, then she flung open the next door.

The bedroom looked empty. But deep inside Janey's gut there was a nugget of knowledge, of recognition. Running to the bed, she dropped to her knees and pulled up the counterpane.

'Oh Dad,' she whispered.

Her father – or some remnant of him – lay on his back beneath the bed. He was still in his caveman state, as she last remembered him. He rolled his head towards her at the sound of her voice, his nose almost hitting the saucer that sat next to his head. It was a dish of water for him to lap like a cat, left by someone who knew he was there. Not Bowood – he'd been too sick. It must have been Jakobi again. That was the 'secret project' he had been working on. He'd been discovering the truth.

Janey fought off the burning sensation across the bridge of her nose. Her father was so helplessly sick he couldn't even feed himself, and great clumps of his hair were scattered around him. Whether it had fallen out or he'd pulled it, Janey couldn't say. Didn't want to say. The bare patches of skin were hideously gnarled with knotted veins, and the eyes that now fixed on Janey had whites almost completely scarlet with blood.

'Oh, Dad, what have I done?'

A withered hand crawled across the carpet

towards Janey, and she held it to her face. But her father pulled it away and pointed at his head.

She knew what he wanted to say, but he was wrong.

'You? No, it wasn't you. You were just the brilliant inventor. So brilliant your parents didn't even send you to school, did they? And then you got sick. Because of me. Because I twisted time.'

To her horror, a tear squeezed out from under her father's flickering eyelid, and he clutched at her hand. 'I . . . Sol . . . I didn't . . . know . . .' he whispered, barely more able to communicate than Eve had been.

'I know, Dad – I know! You wouldn't have done that to your own brother. Nobody could think that.'

Janey lay down next to her father so her cheek rested on his hand. 'I've seen Eve, Dad. I went back. I got the message.'

But Boz shook his head, a tiny movement that started off a convulsion throughout his entire sickened body. 'Dying . . .' he croaked.

'No!'

'Want . . . to.' He tried to smile. 'Better.'

Janey finally let the tears flow. She knew what he meant. Her brain worked in the very same way as his. That word 'better' covered all sorts of things. He meant that he would be better off dead than half alive, in this state. That young Boz would get better if old Boz died.

And perhaps that everyone involved in SPI would be better off if they didn't become involved with the organization in the first place.

But Janey knew otherwise. The only person who wanted him dead was Copernicus. Not young Sol. Just Copernicus.

'There's another way,' she whispered, tears dripping on to her father's hand. 'I'm not letting you go. Either of you. You're coming with me.'

Boz tried to shake his head, but the effort was too much. With all her strength, and the help of her Girl-gauntlet, Janey pulled him out from under the bed and laid him across her ASPIC. 'I can't believe you've been hiding here all this time. Back in a second,' she said, and she ran downstairs.

She unlocked the lounge door and stood firm as Lancelot Brown flounced over from the phone. 'The police are on their way, and—'

'Grandad,' said Janey, holding up her hand to silence him, 'will you help us?'

'Grandad?' said Lancelot quickly. 'Us?'

Janey took his hand and led him up the stairs, throwing open both bedroom doors. 'Oh my life,' he gasped, his hand on his chest. 'There are two of them. That disgusting sea creature and some sort of . . . *caveman*?'

'There isn't time to explain,' said Janey, 'but you know that your family has always been . . .

189

special? Well, they're more special than you realize. These were once your sons.'

Lancelot opened his mouth to protest.

'Trust me!' she begged. 'That one,' she said, nodding towards the caveman, 'is Boz – and he's my dad. We need your help.'

For a moment she thought Lancelot was going to erupt in rage, but instead he clutched the door frames of the bedrooms, one by one, then turned to Janey with an expression so aghast that he seemed to have aged ten years at once. 'So if he's my son *and* he's your father . . . that must make you – dare I say it – my granddaughter?' Janey smiled and nodded sheepishly. 'You do look like a Brown,' he observed.

'So you'll believe me? Can I fill you in later, Gramps? For now I just really really need you to take us to school – and please, no more questions!'

'Well, my girl, the police will be here any second,' he said. 'So let's get going. Where's Carm- . . . your . . . dare I say it . . . grandmother?'

'In the cellar, asleep.'

'Leave her there. Safe. Can you manage Bowood?' He stepped back as Janey took hold of the ASPIC so her father dangled from it like a scarecrow. 'I'll bring the squ- . . . Solomon. Oh my boy, is it really you?' he whispered as he levered Copernicus's broken body off the bed. 'My poor dear boys.'

Between them they managed to manhandle the brothers down the stairs. 'We'll put them in the trailer behind the tractor,' said Lancelot. 'Then they can lie flat. Will the tractor be fast enough? We can go across country.'

Janey thought about its unique tyre. 'I don't think that will be a problem,' she said, and she climbed in the back between the two men, crouching down to make sure she could still hear their breathing, laboured though it was. As her grandfather drove the tractor out of the field, she took hold of her father's hand. After a slight pause, she reached for a tentacle arm and held Copernicus's hand too. 'I'm sorry,' she whispered to the pair. 'Don't die.' And she said it again and again in a sort of prayer until they pulled up at Everdene.

It was too much effort, and too much for the brothers to take, to do anything other than lurch straight through the hall doors, up the stairs and on to the stage. Feathers and splinters and dust clouded the hall, and Janey had to peer through the gloom to make out any of her SPI teams. Her caveman father floated next to her, held up by the ASPIC but not able even to lift his head; nearby, Janey's grandfather, looking bewildered but obedient, was half carrying, half dragging the Squid Man on to the stage.

Janey's heart sank still further at what she could see in the hall. The spy-ring force field had held off some of the enemy spies, and beneath it Gina Bellarina and Rosie Biggenham were back to back, high-kicking at anything and everything that came near. But Alfie had crawled out, over to his mother, who was cornered by a trio of trumpeting hippos, and from the footprints on his back it looked as though he'd been trampled. To what extent, Janey couldn't see, but he was not moving. Gina had managed to stay away from Geneva so was still looking quite perky, but Maisie had gone against Jane's advice and leaped to Mrs Halliday's rescue, and so the older SPI was slumping further and further down the wall, the hippos closing in.

G-Mamma was being carried down the hall by Bert, who had taken off his hat and laid it on G-Mamma's stomach. Overhead, Maddy kicked and pooed a path through the melee, while Trouble slashed wildly at anything near, yowling like a banshee.

Janey hung on to her father, not knowing which way to turn. G-Mamma being carried like that could only mean one thing. She couldn't even think about it. Her beloved SPI:KE, her dear friend and educator, was . . . was . . .

'No!' screamed Janey, scrabbling on the floor for the dropped SPI-Pod. 'No! Stop now! Stop it!'

All heads turned towards her, just as they had when as a new Spylet she'd leaped on to the table to divert the Sinerlesse and rescue her father. So little had changed. She was still trying to save her father, and now everyone else as well, but the enemy was still running amok, tracking her down, killing and maiming and destroying everything she loved and needed . . .

But not any more. Because one thing *had* changed since those early Spylet days. She had. Janey Brown. She was so much Jane Blonde now, and Jane Blonde was her, that there was no difference. Everything and nothing. She was that same black/light column. Janey Brown. Jane Blonde. The same backwards and forwards. Daughter, friend and Spylet.

And she had to make the difference.

Janey beckoned her grandfather across the stage and he staggered over, supporting Copernicus. 'Look at this,' said Janey quietly. 'Our leader,' and she pointed to Boz, 'and yours.' Copernicus was an especially pitiful sight, his ravaged body seeming to be the sum of many parts, but parts that did not – should not – belong together.

As she watched, her caveman father lifted his head for one minuscule moment, then slumped down. Janey felt her heart burst open, even as she heard his younger self take in a deep breath nearby. Boz was better. It could mean only one thing. It was over. Her father was dead. G-Mamma was gone. It was over. Her life as a spy, her friendships, even the new family she'd found – none of that mattered. She would sacrifice it all to get back the lives of the people around her. Even the evil ones.

'This is what we've done.' Tears flowing freely down her face, Janey looked down on the shattered scene of battle, hardly able to recognize the school hall of peaceful hymn-singing and assemblies, or the sweet-natured faces of her friends. 'What are we fighting for?'

'Copernicus!' roared someone from the back of the crowd, and everyone turned to stare at Solomon. 'Justice. That's what we're fighting for.'

'That's not what you really want, is it?' she shouted, and all heads turned her way. 'Not really. It's not what *I* want. I thought I wanted . . . spying, and having an interesting life, and being Jane Blonde. But I can't have one life and have the other too.'

G-Mamma's procession had come to a halt at her feet, and Janey's voice caught in her throat. 'Rosie . . .' she croaked.

'I'm here!' Rosie Biggenham swept through the crowd under the force field, then stopped abruptly at the sight of G-Mamma. 'Oh lordy. Oh lordy lordy lordy.'

Janey took a deep breath. 'Is everything ready?'

Rosie's eyes brightened. 'Yes, Blonderella. G-Mamma helped me organize it . . . for you.'

'Lights,' she said loudly, and Rosie scrambled for the light switch.

The remaining lights flooded the huge hall with brightness, and the restless crowd blinked at each other, looking this way and that, wondering what was going on.

Janey's heart hammered in her chest. She could hardly believe what she was going to do next. It would be the end of everything. The end of Jane Blonde. Maybe even the end of Janey Brown. Or no . . . It would just be that there'd be no beginning. She wouldn't ever exist. Jane Blonde would never even *be*. Janey Brown would either be trapped here forever, growing old at the same rate as her parents . . . or of course, if her parents never really met . . . Jane Blonde would end. And Janey Brown would never begin. She raised her head.

'S. P. I. members – SPIs.' Waiting until all the SPI team were watching her – those who could still see – she nodded at the middle of the room, and then she threw back her head and roared: 'EMOC!'

'Come back!' screamed Solomon. 'She means come back. Stop them!'

But the SPI team had already moved as one, gathering in the centre of the hall, even Alfie, dragged along by his sobbing mother, and G-Mamma's body, still held by Bert and his Spy-pet entourage. Solomon, raving, hauled young Boz towards them, but Janey didn't stop him, though Bowood was fighting back now. She wanted Solomon too.

Did she really want it? Because it wouldn't just be the end of everything she knew as a spy . . .

But time was up. She thought she saw a pair of pale blue eyes shoot past the end of the stage stairs, and for a split second Janey almost stopped – what if her father had made some new invention? And the Spyclops in her pocket – it looked so like the eyes. What if she didn't have to do this? But then she looked at her father's hand in hers, at the palm with its message on it: B4 EVE. Yet another version of her father wouldn't help. It had to end.

Well, that was it. 'Before Eve!' she yelled, in the hope that someone – one of her friends, anyone – would understand why she was doing what she was about to do. 'Rosie, in the middle!'

And then she turned to her grandfather, saying, 'You too,' and pushed the body of her father along on the ASPIC towards the centre of the room, at the same time as she started up the music, and the lights behind the mirrors lining the hall burst into life. 'Look at yourselves,' she cried out. 'See what we've become!' And everyone looked . . . stared at their battered and bloody reflections, puzzled.

Just as she'd intended them to do.

And Janey Brown screamed at the top of her voice, echoing through the SPI-Pod, reaching the ceiling and the far corners and every spy in the room:

'SOLOMON'S POLIFICATIONAL INVESTI-GATORS – I DESPISE YOU!'

Their heads whipped round as she prepared to

launch herself through the air, ready to join them. 'I DESPISE YOU ALL! COPERNICUS, I DESPISE YOU. AND SINERLESSE, AND PAULETTE, AND EVERYONE. EVERY SINGLE ONE OF YOU – YOU ARE ALL . . . DE . . . SPIED!' She Fleet-feet jumped off the stage.

The room shimmered and swam before Janey's eyes. She felt exactly as she had in the BELIEVƎ machine – everything and nothing. In the body of the hall, there was a heart-stopping moment when the spies realized what she had done and then . . .

. . . bodies started disappearing like soap bubbles bursting.

Alfie. Gone. In the blink of an eye.

Janey sobbed, still sailing through the air.

Tish. Leaf, and Rook, then Blackbird. The Spylets. All the Spylets who would not exist if SPI was never invented, if the creator was DeSpied.

And as she watched herself and the others in the DeSpies-U mirror that Rosie had assembled from G-Mamma's gadgetry, Copernicus was snuffed out, and then Gina, and her father . . . the broken body of her father . . . gone, like a kiss blown across a room . . . Those mysterious blue eyes followed her even into non-existence.

Ceasing to exist was probably a lot like dying, Janey thought dreamily, only without the pain. Only now did she notice that the school's name was an anagram. Never end. Everdene/Neverend. Nice. Somehow never beginning meant that she would never end either. SPI would never end. Her father and mother and Alfie and all those she loved – they'd never end. And she smiled vaguely at the pale blue eyes over her shoulder, reflected back at her in the mirror, strangely not attached to any person but floating, floating, and she allowed herself to be dragged upwards . . . upwards . . . ever upwards . . . waiting for her bubble to burst . . . waiting . . . to never be created . . . forever . . . for never . . .

the birthday

'Wake up, sleepyhead.'

A female voice penetrated Janey Brown's dream. She was an angel. Or someone . . . there was an angel there, anyway, with blue eyes and glasses and a hand tugging her ponytail, or possibly the back of her SPIsuit . . .

Janey's eyes flew open. SPIsuit? How did she remember that? She'd DeSpied and ceased to be and probably shouldn't remember having been a Spylet. And who was that, flicking her ear?

Jean Brown's face loomed into view. 'I've never known you sleep in so late. I suppose we'll have to get used to that, now you're another year older.'

'Older?' Janey sat up, trying not to stare too hard at her mum, who looked like she normally did, only better. Like she'd had a makeover.

Jean rolled her eyes. 'That was a heck of a sleep. You haven't even remembered it's a special day.

Well, happy birthday, darling.' Her mum kissed Janey on the forehead and then on each cheek. 'And you'd better get up. Everyone's arriving for your birthday lunch in less than an hour.'

'Everyone?'

Jean shook her head, laughing. 'Are you a changeling? Who took my chatty daughter and replaced her with One-Word Girl? Everyone – all your cousins, and your aunts and uncles, and . . .' She arched an eyebrow mischievously. 'Dad's got your present downstairs.'

'Dad?' Janey shouted it as if she'd never heard the word before, nearly falling out of bed.

'There you go again,' said her mother

'Yours or mine?' blurted Janey. 'Your dad or my dad?'

'Well, mine's still dead,' said Jean slowly. 'Skiing accident when I was young. Remember?'

'My dad then. My dad's got my present. Downstairs. Now.' Janey knew she was babbling, but it was all very confusing.

Jean sat down on the bed. 'Are you all right, Janey?'

'I think,' said Janey, hugging her hard, 'that I'm probably very all right.'

'OK. Well, put something nice on, and I'll see you downstairs.'

Janey leaped out of bed the minute her mum had

left the room. First she ran over to the mirror. Janey Brown looked back at her, although, like her mum, she was a glossier, perkier version of herself, with sleek dark-blonde hair and alert, intelligent eyes dancing in the reflection. 'Wow,' said Janey, then she ran to the fireplace. She tapped at the ten past two position, and then at quarter past three, and then right round the fireplace in a circle, but there was no grinding noise from the back of the grate. Which meant there was no Spylab on the other side of the wall, and no G-Mamma.

Janey sat back on her heels. No G-Mamma. That was going to be hard to get her head around. There would forever be an aching space in her life. But there was someone downstairs she had to see. She blew a kiss into the fireplace, vowing to bring some fake SPI-buys up as a memorial, then opened the bedroom door.

The house was normal. Smart, and better furniture, but normal-ish. More like Janey remembered it than it had been in Geneva's time, but still home. She smiled at the framed family tree hanging at the top of the landing, then skipped down the stairs.

In the hallway an attack of nerves suddenly gripped her insides. Her dad. She'd never before come down to her dad, her own real, normal dad. Her spy dad, yes. Dad the caveman, yes. But who was this one going to be?

201

There was only one way to find out. Gingerly Janey pushed open the door.

And there he was. Boz. It was Boz, blue-eyed and dark-haired and healthy and . . . fine. Normal again! Janey nearly burst out laughing, but then remembered that, to her parents, this was a special day only because it was her birthday. Not because it was the day she discovered she actually *did* exist, that her mother and father had got together and married and had a baby, and that the baby was her – Janey Brown.

Janey rushed over and wrapped her arms around him. It didn't matter anyway. Here he was. Right in her home.

'Happy birthday,' said her father, laughing and gasping as she squeezed the breath out of him. 'You'll have to have them more often if I get hugs like that!'

Janey grinned at him, speechless with joy.

'I suppose you want your present?' Boz waited for her to nod, then said, 'Gina, honey, do you want to do the honours?'

Gina! She called herself Gina, not Jean. Janey could see why. She suited it very well. Her mum opened the back door and scooped something off the floor, then stepped up beside Boz, hiding her hands behind him. 'One, two, three . . . Happy birthday!'

'Oh! He's gorgeous!'

It was a kitten, scrawny and tawny with an

oversized tail and large, blinking, hypnotic eyes. 'I'm going to call him T—'

'Trouble!' said her parents in unison. She'd obviously said it before. In fact, Janey thought, if she'd been going on about getting a cat named Trouble, maybe the whole spy past was just something else she'd wished for.

She tickled the kitten under the chin. 'Tiny Trouble, I was going to say.' She peered up at her dad innocently. 'So, Dad, are you going to work today?'

Boz took a hefty bite of his bacon sandwich. It looked great. Dad must do the cooking, thought Janey. 'Even quantum physicists get Saturdays off, Janey,' he said cheerily, 'especially when it's their daughter's birthday.'

Hmmm. Quantum physics. Sounded boring. She'd have to find out more about it, but right now it seemed that everything about her family was resoundingly everyday. Normal. Which was . . . nice, Janey decided, although she couldn't help feeling a slight twinge of something that felt a little like disappointment. Life would really not ever be the same again.

Suddenly there was the blast of a car horn. Boz grinned at Gina. 'They're early. Again.'

'Honestly.' Gina shoved a trayful of sausage rolls into the oven and wiped her hands. 'Auntie Maisie can't resist keeping to a timetable. She'd give the Queen detention for being late.'

Janey swivelled on her chair, bacon hanging out of her mouth. 'Auntie Maisie?'

'Open the door then,' said Gina.

Auntie Maisie! Auntie Maisie? How could that be? Was it a coincidence? Janey wrenched open the door even before the doorbell finished dinging, and there on the doorstep stood Mrs Halliday, hand not even back down at her side. 'Happy birthday,' she said, grinning broadly with teeth that were pearly and well-shaped with not a hint of jaggedness about them. She pecked Janey on the cheek and stepped into the hall, and the tall figure behind her bent to give Janey a hug and a birthday wish too.

The voice was deep, and horribly familiar, and Janey swallowed down a gulp as she looked up into the handsome face of Copernicus. He frowned. 'OK?'

Trying not to stare, Janey checked his lip. It was whole. His hair was thick and glossy, and brushed against his collar. It didn't look to be at all the kind of hair that Mrs Halliday would approve of. Janey nodded. It was all she could trust herself to do.

Maisie laughed. 'Sol, don't tease her. Let her cousin hand over the present.'

Solomon pulled her ponytail gently and followed his wife down the hall, leaving Janey to face her cousin on the doorstep.

Alfie stuck out his hand with a package in it. When Janey just stood gawping at him, he pulled her hand open and wedged the parcel in it. 'It's an i-Pod,' he whispered. 'Don't worry – I chose the music.'

'Thanks,' squeaked Janey.

Alfie rolled his dark eyes, so exactly like his father's. 'Are you going to let me in? You're not . . .' His face screwed up tight. 'You're not expecting me to give you a kiss too, are you? Cos that's, like, gross.'

'No,' said Janey, although she felt like hugging him to bits. It was perfect! No wonder they'd been such good friends. They were cousins! Related! Her family was so much bigger than she'd imagined, and it was filled with the most wonderful people. And she knew exactly how to handle Alfie. 'As if. I was just going to slam the door in your face.'

'Try it,' said Alfie, mocking.

Janey shoved the door closed and they tussled for a moment, but then she waited till he was pushing really hard and let the door swing open. Alfie stumbled through the doorway into the hall on to his knees, then brushed himself down. 'OK. That makes the score four–three. To me. And I'll get you next time, JB.'

Laughing, Janey watched him as he walked into the kitchen, slapping his father amiably on the back as he suffered a kiss from Gina. 'Brilliant,' she whispered. She was about to shut the door when there was another honk of a horn from the street.

'Uncle James!'

She'd forgotten that she already had an uncle –

205

one that she did actually see from time to time. Her cousins were a different matter though, and Janey felt suddenly a little shy again as Edie and Fen, the fashion twins, sauntered up the path in trendy outfits, the like of which Uncle James had never allowed her to buy when she was staying with him.

'Hi, Janey! Happy birthday,' they carolled together, handing Janey a bag like Edie's and some hairclips like Fen's as they swept into the house.

Janey stared after them, puzzled. 'I've forgotten which one's which,' she said apologetically to Uncle James.

He smiled, screwing up his face as he polished his glasses. 'I do that all the time,' he admitted in his whiny, nasal voice. 'I don't think they notice. Trust me to have got a bargain, even with the kids. Two for the price of one!'

So he hadn't changed. Still thinking about business and the cost of everything. Janey gave him a kiss on the cheek and waved him into the kitchen.

Everyone was here. Well, nearly everyone. 'Happy birthday, Janey,' she whispered to herself, and with a last longing glance over the hedge to next door she went and joined her party.

emoc

All afternoon they chatted and laughed and ate, spilling out into the garden as the day got warmer and the kitchen started to feel cramped. Janey admired Alfie's choice of music, and showed off about it a little to Edie and Fen (or Fen and Edie) and stared sneakily at her parents and Maisie and Sol whenever she got the opportunity.

She was standing in the kitchen on her own, watching Solomon Brown laughing at something his son had said, and wondering how he had turned out so nice – or rather, hadn't turned out so horrible – when Uncle James strolled into the kitchen with a bottle of beer in his hand. 'Empty,' he said, waggling it at her. 'No more for me. Driving.'

'Sensible,' said Janey, nodding.

He laughed. 'I am, aren't I? Not like that lot.' They stood side by side for a moment, gazing out into the garden, smiling and nodding at the general feelings of niceness that abounded on the patio. Then suddenly Uncle James cleared his throat.

'I don't think I ever told you how much I enjoyed having you to stay with me, Jane,' he said, scratching his chin. 'We should do that more often.'

Janey nodded, wondering what to say. Staying with Uncle James had actually been very peculiar, and she wasn't in any hurry to repeat the experience. But then he spoke again, saving her from the task. 'Oh, silly me! I forgot to give you your present.'

'But I got a bag, and hair things . . .'

'Those are from the girls. This is something special.' Uncle James smiled down at her. 'I hear you like pets.'

Janey nodded slowly. What was going on?

'It's in the car. Tell you what,' said Uncle James cheerfully, 'meet me on the landing in a minute.'

'Landing?'

'You'll see!' Uncle James turned and grinned at her as he sauntered down the path, walking with his parting into the wind, and Janey's breath caught in her throat. He looked . . . different. Confident. And his voice had changed too. Instead of sounding like he was speaking underwater, his voice was big and booming. The kind of voice that could reach the back of a school hall, could be the compère at a fashion show, would make a great Head Boy. 'Jakobi Delacroix!' whispered Janey, remembering.

Weird, she thought, dashing up the stairs as instructed. She studied the family tree as she waited. There he was, right next to Geneva, with a little line going out to the side to his ex-wife, and another going down to the twins' names. And suddenly he was right behind her.

'Oh! I didn't hear you. How did you creep up on me like that?'

'Trick of the trade.' Uncle James grinned, a flash of white teeth against his golden skin. His blue eyes were merry behind his glasses. 'Here,' he said, and put a large cardboard box at her feet.

Janey crouched down. 'I . . . I've seen this before,' she said, trying to think where.

She eased the lid open, amazed at what was inside. 'Bob!' It was the tortoise, his name still etched on his shell. 'He's still . . . is this the original Bob?'

'They live to a ripe old age,' said Uncle James, sitting on the landing next to her. 'Either that, or they time-travel.' He laughed. 'Oh, gosh, look what else I left in there.' He fished a small sandy marble out of the straw and dropped it into his pocket.

Suddenly he took off his glasses and winked at Janey, and the brightness of his pale blue eyes made her jaw drop. 'You do remember, don't you, Janey?' he said softly in his new deep, confident voice.

And at once Janey made sense of all she had seen. Blue eyes floating by. Blue eyes, rescuing

209

her. Pulling her back from the DeSpies-U. 'You!' She couldn't believe it. 'How did you know? How did you do it? How . . . ?' She stammered to a stop, lost for words.

Uncle James smiled again. 'Well, I told you I was following you, didn't I? Couldn't let Geneva have all the fun. Right from the fashion show, I followed you around. When you dropped by with young Alfie there, I planted a Spyclops in the room so I could hear all about what you were up to – I think you stood on it on the way out – and then I put on Alfie's Invisibubble, made sure your dad had water, and then went to the hall. Spent a very happy hour or so punching people without them being able to see me, and then when you came back and tried to de-spy everyone I jumped around through time a bit and left a few messages and then I—'

'You! You pulled me out of the hall, and . . .'

'Brought you back up the BELIEVƎ slide. Much easier for me to make the journey with the Invisibubble on. You were a bit spacey though.' And Uncle James ruffled her hair.

Janey didn't know what to think. Uncle James. Boring, business-brained Uncle James. He'd done this amazing thing – several amazing things – and now he was talking about them just as if he was talking to her mother about Jean's Clean Machines.

She remembered something. 'Does that mean . . .

ages ago, when I first became a . . . a you know what . . . I came to your bank, because G-Mamma had turned up and . . .'

'Yes, thank you for that. Unfortunately I'd had to disappear pretty quickly, and your mum got into trouble instead. Trapped by the Sinerlesse. But I knew exactly who to call.' Uncle James got up and stretched his legs, looming over her on the landing, and she was suddenly aware that he was not at all nerdy and skinny.

It was unbelievable. 'Does that mean you're a . . . you're a . . . ?'

Uncle James laughed. 'I certainly don't do bank work as my main job. Just did that when I took my English name on – James Delocroix. To sound like a finance man. But really – I sort of went into the family business.' He nodded towards the family tree behind him. 'If you're interested, I'll be in touch. If you ever want to . . . EMOC.'

Janey stood too, dashing over to the family tree as Uncle James coughed, tried out his whiny voice for size and headed off down the stairs. What did he mean about the family business? Tracing the line with her finger, she worked up from the twins. Edie and Fen Delacroix. Up to James – Jakobi Delacroix. Then up to the next level – her mum's and James's parents, who were also her grandparents . . . Monique the Unique Delacroix – that was right, they'd been brought up by Monique's parents. And Monique was married to

. . . Janey's finger trailed across. Andrew Bond. Which would mean that Jakobi Delacroix's name would be . . .

'No way!' shouted Janey.

But before she had time to ask him, there was a knock at the door. 'You get that, Janey!' shouted Uncle James, nasal again.

Janey raced down the stairs, not sure if she could take any more surprises. She opened the door, and nearly fainted.

There was a woman on the doorstep. She was large and bubbly with round blue eyes caked in make-up, and she was dressed as an octopus.

'Janey Brown?' she said brightly.

Janey nodded, hardly daring to breathe.

'HAPPY BIRTHDAY!' hollered the woman. 'I'm your singing telegram, sent by . . .' She studied the piece of paper in her hand. '. . . Uncle James. I think he wrote this himself,' she whispered confidentially. 'It's the sort of rubbish uncles do. Anyway!'

And she leaped back up the path, pressed a switch on her portable CD player and gyrated her hips vigorously. Janey knew – she hoped she knew – what was coming, and she was right. Rosie Biggenham burst into verse.

'My name's Rosie B and I'm here to say,
You'd better get your booty underway.

The party's in the kitchen and it's plain to see
It's a very happy birthday for Janey B!
Who's the happy birthday girl?
Janey B! Ha-a-ave fun!'

She pointed a dazzling fingernail at Janey and she sauntered off down the path, waving her tentacles.

Janey hardly dared to breathe. Was it her? Could it really be her SPI:KE? She'd called herself Rosie B, so at least she was definitely Rosie Biggenham, but on this weird and wonderful day, was there any chance . . .?

The woman had reached the gate.

Janey opened her mouth. 'G-M . . .' She swallowed. 'G-Mamma.'

The rotund octopus stopped, then turned around slowly. 'Well. Lordy lordy lordy.' A smile spread over her face. 'I haven't been called that in a very, very long time. Since I was a –' She sighed nostalgically – 'a singing sensation.'

Janey's heart, which had risen into her throat, plumped back into her stomach. It was her stage name. Not her spy-name.

The round face contemplated her for a moment, then G-Mamma put the CD player on the floor and punched one of the buttons. 'Perhaps you remember this one,' she said softly, and stuck three tentacles in the air.

The music started. As the woman started to sing a crowd gathered in the porch behind Janey.

'Spylets are forever.
They can transform in the Wower,
Run at miles and miles an hour.
They do missions at night
With permission to fight evil power . . .'

'That's not how it goes,' said Maisie Halliday. 'Alfie, come back inside. Don't stare at the poor woman.'

G-Mamma was in full flight with the second verse. The more people stared at her, the more energetic her performance became.

'Spylets are forever.
Take a special one and train her.
Give her gadgets to sustain her.
Tie her ponytail high, 'gainst the villains who try
To detain her.

Give me Jane Blonde!
For Blonde is the Spylet . . .
Fleet-feet to Girl-gauntlet.
When all hope is gone,
Jane Blonde spies on!'

Her voice hit an ear-splitting crescendo, and Janey

fought back tears. The crowd behind her shuffled away uncomfortably one by one, until there was only herself standing there, and Uncle James lurking down the hall.

'OK, bossy boss-man?' shouted G-Mamma. 'I hadn't finished! Some people don't appreciate talent.'

'I know. Get on with it, Rosie,' replied Janey's uncle in his deep voice, before he trotted back down the hall.

G-Mamma stared at Janey for a long, long moment. Then she angled her head and looked along the road. 'Are you coming then, Blonde? Or do I have to stand around dressed like Mrs Copper Knickers all day . . . Grab your cat, and let's splat.'

And Janey Brown threw back her shiny ponytail, and laughed till she cried.

THE END

acknowledgements

At the end of this journey, or this section of this journey, I don't really know where to start to thank all the people who've waved me off confidently from the beginning, directed me at crossroads, taken my hand across the rocky sections, helped me pick up the rubbish and recycle it along the way and given me metaphorical hugs as the end of the road draws near. but here goes:

Glenys, we just wouldn't be here without you. Janey, Jane and I are eternally grateful for your endless patience, constant wisdom and super-necessary straight talking. you are the ace among agents and the finest of friends.

Rachel, your enthusiasm and expertise brought JB to life. how dare you be so young and so gosh-darn brilliant?! Miss you, and will never forget that this girl is as much yours as mine. And talking of young and brilliant – Emma, you stuck that baton into the crook of your elbow and set off at a pace. You let me get away with nothing, and for that and your wonderful guidance I thank you endlessly. Here's to much more . . .

To the other Macmillan folk who have helped JB (and me) grow, you are the most wonderful work colleagues: Jane, John, and OE Angie in NZ; Dom and Talya and Other Emma and everyone in the UK, I had the great privilege to meet up with you all during the creation of *Spylets Are Forever*, and you have helped in so many ways I couldn't possibly count them. Cheers, buddies.

For the friends who've packed me off to work when I'd rather drink coffee, who've helped me out when it should have been the other way round and who've kept me sane (well, it's all relative) even from the other end of the planet: RESPECT. I can't name you all for fear of missing someone out, but you know who you are, and you're all brilliant.

Katie, you make me laugh every single day and sometimes I steal the things that have made me laugh and put them in these books. One day you'll see! Love, love, love. And Mum and Dad, my first audience and source of endless support, thank you times a million.

To Lucy Dahlenburg, huge gratitude and G-Mamma doughnuts due for letting me pinch the word 'smuffocate'.

And last but not least . . . in fact, first (read the book – you CAN be first and last at the same time!), to all those lovely Spylets who have told me what Jane (or G-Mamma, or Alfie, or Trouble . . .) means to them, well, you mean every bit as much to me. May you all find your inner Blonde; to the unexpected boy fans (e.g. Christopher Roberts and Matthew Torckler), soooo well done for not judging a book by its cover; to the dedicated Spylets who have tracked me down in person – Agents Morning, Lolo McBobo, Hideaway, Evie C., your names spring to mind!; to the wonderful people who've mailed me and given me ideas and volunteered to play Jane (or G-Mamma, or Alfie, or Trouble . . .) in any film versions – keep reading, keep your spying eyes peeled and, most of all, keep being marvellous. because after all . . . SPYLETS ARE FOREVER. xx

PREPARE TO MEET JACK.

HE'S . . . BARKING.

Jack ran his tongue along his lower teeth as he jogged back to Lowmount. Then the upper. Then he moaned. His canines were enormous. Dog-like. He actually wished he was at the dentist, having them pulled out.

After a while he broke into a trot, trying to avoid being distracted by the enticing scents drifting up from the surrounding trees and plants – cat, and hedgehog (which made him turn a little giddy and run around in a circle, scrabbling around on the ground for a moment, but he couldn't see the prickly creature and eventually remembered what he was meant to be doing). Most of all, what he could smell was other dogs. No! Not other dogs. Dogs. 'I'm a boy,' he said to himself. 'Not a dog. A kid. A normal boy. Well, maybe not normal, but . . . yes! A normal-ish boy.'

At length he emerged from the hedgerow behind the tall limestone columns of the folly, and he took a quick glance in the ornamental pond. He was still hairy. Still snub-nosed and black. Still very much a freak, he was sad to observe. As he rubbed at a patch of the coarse black hair on his cheek Jack stopped and looked at his hand. At least that wasn't hairy. It was a bit of a funny colour, slightly bluey-black, as if he'd been rolling in dirt. But then he remembered that he *had* been rolling in dirt, at the near-delight of finding a hedgehog, and couldn't decide whether or not the memory made him feel any better.

One thing was certain, however. He could not go into detention – or anywhere, for that matter – looking like this. With a deep sigh Jack tacked up the sloping ground towards the Hall and scooted down the corridor, frantically trying to turn back at the ominous click of his mother's heels on the parquet flooring.

It was too late. She'd heard him.

'Jack? Is that you? What are you doing home?' *Click click. Click click. Click click click click click.*

She was nearly upon him. Jack touched his face in despair, then grabbed the helmet from a nearby suit of armour. He shoved it quickly over his ears and rammed it down, the visor not quite closing over the extra length of his nose. Leaning against the wall, he raised a hand nonchalantly as his mother loomed into view.

'Jack Algernon Bootle-Cadogan, what on earth are you doing?'

Think, Jack, think! he told himself. 'Er . . . just popped back for this,' he said thickly, pointing at the helmet. 'We're doing the Civil War in history; thought

I'd show everyone an original Royalist helmet.'

'Oh, Jack!' His mother hurried over and cuddled him to her cashmere cardigan, Jack nearly vomiting at the overpowering aroma of Hermès perfume. And at being clutched to the bosom of his cool and distant mother. 'You've never shown any enthusiasm for our heritage before. Furthermore, I wouldn't have thought the hoi polloi at Clearwell would be at all interested in our patriotic past. How lovely!' She rapped his visor. 'I would have thought it would be better to hand it around though, not wear it. Take it off.' And she started tugging at the helmet to prise it from his head.

'No!' shouted Jack, hanging on for dear life.

Find out how it all began . . .

Jane Blonde

'Until now, you have been just plain old Janey Brown. But you are going to grow and grow. You will be what your parents have not allowed you to be. It's in your past. And it's in your future. There's a whole new part of you just waiting to you to burst out. You are Jane Blonde – Sensational Spylet. Welcome to our world.'

Follow Jane Blonde on her first non-stop mission!

Jane Blonde
spies trouble

Jane's purr-ecious spy-cat, Trouble, has been kidnapped! A group of mad scientists think they have discovered the secret to a cat's nine lives – but they need Trouble for their experiments. All the clues lead down the drain – spying can be a wet and stinky business! But with chewing gum that lets her breathe underwater, a SPIpod tracking device and a high-speed mini-hover-board, Jane Blonde is ready for ACTION . . .

Jane Blonde
twice the splyet

Jane Blonde, Sensational Spylet, has just met her secret twin!

When the sisters are posted to an Australian sheep farm, Janey's instincts are on red alert. There's something weird about those sheep. Come to think of it, there's something suspicious about Jane Blonde's twin . . .

Janey can raise an invisible shield with her spy-ring and she can burrow through the earth with her spy-drill boots – but will incredible gadgets save her this time?

Jane Blonde
spylet on ice

Jane Blonde, Sensational Spylet, is hurled on her coolest mission yet when she enrols at SPIcamp!

There are gadgets galore at the top-secret facility and there's even a snowdome where the spylets can chill out. And when the team is sent on a mysterious polar expedition, Janey's spylet-training – and her new snowboard skills! – are put to the test.

Jane Blonde
goldenspy

Janey is delighted when she is granted a dazzling
golden spysuit. But things get deadly serious
when her investigations lead her to a shocking
discovery: her arch enemy has developed a
terrible giant Lay-Z Beam, which he is directing
at Earth from a secret space station! Will the
Goldenspy manage to resist its zapping power
– and save the world?

Jane Blonde
spy in the sky

When Jane Blonde becomes a sky-diving sensation, she's on cloud nine! But her flying skills are put to the test when a flock of freaky creatures takes to the air.

Can Blonde uncover the dangerous force behind her new enemy before she's blasted out of the skies?

A selected list of titles available from Macmillan Children's Books

The prices shown below are correct at the time of going to press. However, Macmillan Publishers reserves the right to show new retail prices on covers, which may differ from those previously advertised.

JILL MARSHALL

Jane Blonde, Sensational Spylet	978-0-330-43814-8	**£5.99**
Jane Blonde Spies Trouble	978-0-330-43825-4	**£5.99**
Jane Blonde, Twice the Spylet	978-0-330-44657-0	**£5.99**
Jane Blonde, Spylet on Ice	978-0-330-44658-7	**£5.99**
Jane Blonde, Goldenspy	978-0-230-53244-1	**£5.99**
Jane Blonde, Spy in the Sky	978-0-330-45812-2	**£5.99**
Jane Blonde, Spylets Are Forever	978-0-330-45813-9	**£5.99**

All Pan Macmillan titles can be ordered from our website, www.panmacmillan.com, or from your local bookshop and are also available by post from:

Bookpost, PO Box 29, Douglas, Isle of Man IM99 1BQ

Credit cards accepted. For details:
Telephone: 01624 677237
Fax: 01624 670923
Email: bookshop@enterprise.net
www.bookpost.co.uk

Free postage and packing in the United Kingdom